The [mis]Adventures of
Unan the Conqueror
and
the Princess of Havok

A collection of short stories
By C.M. Rizal

This book is a work of fiction. Names, characters, places, and incidents are products of the author's imagination or are used fictitiously. Any resemblance to actual events or locales or person, living or dead, is entirely coincidental.

Published by Blue Star Press, Canton, MI.
ISBN: 978-0-6151-5194-6

For my Silly Girl

| Happiness and Confusion

A small, public school. Unan stands at her locker, holding a banana. The enemy constantly walks past, giggling and pointing at her as she waits for her sidekick. Alert eyes watch down the hallway. A disgruntled Princess of Havok finally shows up, wearing the usual: gray skirt, white blouse, sweater vest, striped socks, and combat boots.

"I hate school," she growls. Her bag is flung across the hallway and her arms across her stomach.

"Smile!" Unan cries, giddily. She waves her banana in the air, and a few of the enemy stop to stare.

"Fuckers!" Princess of Havok yells, knowing they're behind her. They leave, slowly. "Blue hair," she comments, pointing at Unan's head. "New color this week, huh?"

"Yup," Unan replies. "What's going on tomorrow?"

"Kermie has a soccer game. You going?" she asks, retrieving her bag.

"Yeah... hot guys. Couldn't pass that up. Can I wear your spikes?" she asks. Princess of Havok takes off her bracelet and hands it over.

First Class: Geometry

The teacher drones on and on while the class talks above her. Unan draws the scene, and Princess of Havok writes a letter to her cousin in Canada. She sits slouched, her leg resting on the desk in front of her. A rapper limps up to the front of the classroom, passing by the both of them.

"Hey, baby," he says to Princess of Havok. "Wanna git wid me?"

"Go fuck yourself, you stupid shit-for-brains *asshole*," she mutters, continuing to write. He grabs a hall pass and makes an attempt to spit at her. It lands on her boots, and she becomes very upset, spitting back. "Fuck 'em all." The teacher asks Unan a question. Nobody had been listening.

"Um, e equals mc squared?" she answers, grinning sheepishly.

"Lovely," the teacher replies with a frown, turning back to the messy chalkboard. A wad of gum flies up to the front of the classroom, hitting a spot just above the teacher's head. Only a few people laugh, including Unan and Princess of Havok; the rappers and jocks are sleeping, and the preps are just plain disgusted. Unan turns around, and the skater guy in the back waves, then gives her a thumbs-up sign. She returns the favor, smiling. Princess of Havok raises her eyebrows, and the day goes on.

Second Class: History

They sit in the back, planning revenge on the enemy. Princess of Havok suggests they take over the world; with a bit of strategy and skill, it could easily happen. Or what if Unan's banana was really a flame-thrower? They could torch the school.

The new discussion in class for today is war. It's boring at first, but slowly becomes more and more interesting. War against the enemy... torture the preps... ideas fly through Unan's head. But it wasn't a *real* war... just a war against conformity.

"I think I'm against war," Princess of Havok says aloud, to no one in particular. A few people turn around and tell her to shutup. Unan agrees, nodding her head.

"Yeah, me too." She waves her banana in the air, threatening, loudly, to eat it. The teacher glares at her and continues on with the lecture. Princess of Havok picks away at her desk with a tiny pocketknife. She stares blankly and sighs. Unan wonders what she is thinking and quickly gets her answer.

"I think I'm against *everything*," she announces, stabbing the desk so that the knife stands straight up. She later falls asleep, quietly.

Third Class: The Shit Split

Unan and Princess of Havok have to part for third class, one going to Spanish and the other to English. Princess of Havok treads down the long hallway, and Unan just wanders until it's been ten minutes since the bell rang. Another teacher grabs her and leads her to her room. She always becomes disoriented at this time of the day, losing her sidekick to the army of the enemy. She lets the teacher drag her into a classroom, but she doesn't listen. Unan sits on the floor and doodles, with black permanent marker, on the wall closest to her. She hopes her spikes aren't falling out yet because she wants to show some special people in her Programming class. The teacher mentions that she's not paying attention, and Unan mutters something about "wasted youth." Nothing makes sense already, and the English teacher insists on having philosophical talks with people of the most confused age. Dumb bitch. Unan leans her head against the wall and rolls her eyes, wondering how much time she has left to sit and wait for class to be over with. The bell rings.

The enemy crowds around, fighting to get down the hallway without messing up their clothes, hair, or makeup.

"How was English?" Princess of Havok asks, smiling. She already knows the answer, yet she continues to ask, day in and day out.

"Totally zoned out." A few preps bump into them and continue walking.

"*Delgada* bitches," Princess of Havok replies. Unan's eyes brighten up.

"*Delgada*? You learned something new in Spanish today! I'm so proud of

3

you," she says. Princess of Havok receives a pat on the head. She is grinning from ear to ear, happy that Unan is pleased.

Fourth Class: Programming

"Alexey!!!" Princess of Havok cries, running to him with open arms. They hug, and he moves on to Unan.

"Great spikes!" he comments. "And I thought I told you *never* to call me Alexey!" he says to Princess of Havok, touching the tip of her nose with his finger. She blushes and looks up at him with puppy eyes.

"Sorry, but I couldn't help it... sexy Alexey," she mutters, laughing. Unan cries out.

"Sexy!!! She said sexy!" Dave walks into the classroom later, telling Unan that her spikes are almost the color of his eyes. She waves her banana again, like the baton of a conductor. He grabs it.

"Dave! That's my weapon of mass destruction!" she protests. He holds it out of her reach. The teacher storms in, telling everyone to sit down. For one class, they actually obey. Unan attempts to reach the banana, but it's no use.

"I'm hungry," he replies, simply. She can't argue. He opens it and takes a large bite, slowly breaking it down inside his mouth. He was always so sensual. She watches him eat the whole thing, staring at him in awe and wonder. A giggle comes from next to her. She turns to see Princess of Havok sitting on Alexey's lap.

"But Mr.---" she insists. The teacher shakes his head, and she returns to her seat. Unan turns back to Dave, who is sitting cross-legged at his desk with his chin in his hands. He notices her staring at him.

"Sorry. I'll bring you another one tomorrow," he offers. She shakes her head.

"It's not that."

"What is it?"

"Nothing." Another meaningless conversation; she prefers to simply sit and gaze at him all hour. Princess of Havok waves her hand in front of her face, breaking her concentration.

4

"Programming's the best!" she cries. Unan nods.

"Hell yeah. Friends..." she begins, not finishing.

"Yup. Friends." Alexey and Dave both look at them and smile. Opposite people attracted. They are different; Alexey and Dave somewhat mysterious in nature and spirit, and Unan and Princess of Havok spunky, energetic kids. But screw it. They don't care. They don't give a damn. They are different from the enemy, and that means everything to them.

After school is over, they run down the hallways shrieking, until a janitor tells them they have to go home. Alexey hugs Unan and Princess of Havok, and Dave just smiles. He winks at Unan and whispers into her ear.

"That was a damn good banana. And I'll bring you one tomorrow. See ya later, conqueror." He follows Alexey out the door, his black pants dragging along the floor. Princess of Havok sighs.

"That boy makes me drool," she says, shaking her head. Her hands go onto her hips. "Well, I guess it's time to pack up and go home." For Unan, this means another night slept through at the coffeehouse. She trudges along, passing by more of the enemy. They point and laugh at her.

Secretly, she packs some mud into her hand, holding it behind her back. She walks by.

"Here, bitchy bitchy bitchy," she calls. As she passes, she drops the mud onto their shoes.

"Yuck! I just paid eighty dollars for these!" one cries.

"Sorry, but that's what you get for not shopping at Salvation Army," Unan chimes, in a sing-songy voice. "Come again!" The preps just stare.

"You are such a freak!"

"Thank you. It was nice doing business with you, too," Unan replies. She continues down the street.

The night on the booth seat is quite comfortable, so going to school the next morning isn't as unbearable as usual. Unan gets her clothes from the back room and changes. It's time to see her sidekick once again.

So another day goes by. After school, Unan walks home with Princess of Havok. A rapper passes them.

"Why the hell do you carry a banana every day?" he asks. Unan frowns, becoming angry; nobody is allowed to say anything about the almighty banana!

"What the hell do *you* care, dipshit?" Unan replies. He glares at her.

"You better watch yourself, bitch. Me and my boys got enough ammo to—" Unan is frustrated.

"This ain't no war! What are you gonna do? Blow my head off because I carry around a household fruit?!!" Princess of Havok is slightly frightened. She has never heard Unan speak so fiercely. Perhaps her mind is starting to decay, which one would find hard to believe at so young an age. But what would you expect in a world so fallen apart, so filled with *followers*? What happens when there are no more leaders, no one to take care of the world? Princess of Havok knows it hurts to think sometimes, so she simply pats Unan on the back.

"It'll be okay." A broken promise, a meaningless statement. Everyone says that, but does anyone know for sure?

When they get to the game, Kermie is waiting patiently. He is ready to change into his uniform, and he hands them a bag.

"Watch this for me, kay?" It is a rhetorical question, and neither of them protests. He walks to a small concession building with restrooms in the back. They sit on the light gray bleachers. Unan begins to eat her banana because in school, Dave promised to bring her one every day for the rest of the week. What a sweetheart. A guy walks over to them.

"So the adventure begins," Princess of Havok mumbles. The guy is not too great looking, not too bad looking; not too short, not too tall; not too skinny, not too heavy.

"Hi," he says. He seems quiet. "You know Kevin?"

"Yeah," Unan replies. Princess of Havok is pretty sure she's met this boy before. She has also seen him grinding along a picnic bench with rollerblades. She doesn't mention anything; obviously, he does not remember her. She is somewhat different from what she was like back then.

"I'm Skip," he announces. They look at each other, both wondering how

6

to introduce themselves to him.

"I'm Unan," Unan speaks up. "And this is the Princess of Havok." He laughs, smiling.

"Sure." They all wait for Kermie to return, quietly. Skip begins to hum "Plateau" by Nirvana. Kermie comes back, ready to play.

"I see you met Skip," he says. They begin to walk across the soccer field, slowly.

"Yeah, and I'll find out what your *real* names are!!!" Skip threatens, walking backwards. He turns back around and greets a couple friends from the team.

At half time, Unan and Princess of Havok decide to take a potty break and go explore the woods after that. By the time they return to the soccer field, it's the beginning of the second half of the game. By now, Princess of Havok has taken off her sweater vest because of the heat outside.

"I hope Kermie scores," Princess of Havok comments. They continue to watch. Skip is up in the air, having just headed the ball; a boy from the other team gives a mischievous grin and kicks Skip, sending him awkwardly toward the hard ground. They hear a CRACK, immediately followed by a thump. Everyone is still.

"Bastard!!!" Unan yells loudly, breaking the silence. The part of Skip's leg between his knee and his ankle is bent at a position no human leg should be. The coach runs out and both teams begin to desert the field. The culprit runs over to the supporters, who happen to be seated right next to Unan and Princess of Havok.

"It wasn't me!" he laughs, holding up his hands. "Well, actually... it was!!!" He cannot stop giggling like a madman.

"He's a big kid. I'm sure he was able to handle the fall," an older man says. He glances at his watch.

"Damn, they better hurry up," another man replies.

"I know! I want to get on with the game! But if they forfeit, it's alright. I'm sure we would've won anyways," another boy adds. Princess of Havok shakes her head with a look of disgust on her face, not believing what she

7

hears.

"What the hell is *wrong* with you people?!!" she cries. She doesn't continue because it is too difficult for her. If she were to try and vent her frustration, it would most likely cost someone his or her life. The coach runs over to the sidelines.

"We think he broke his leg. The ambulance is on its way right now," he announces. Both Unan and Princess of Havok feel for Skip; he must be in extreme pain.

"Well, aren't you going to *do* something?" Unan yells.

"There's nothing we can do." Nobody makes an attempt to help Skip in any way. So a body lies in the field, knees bent. The other team members and their parents continue to laugh and chatter.

"I'm tellin' ya, I'm sure he can handle it! He's such a big kid," the older man keeps saying, over and over again. Unan turns to Princess of Havok.

"He's different, like us. We should do something for him. He's *one of us*," Unan says, standing up. "But what can we do?" Princess of Havok quickly makes up her mind to go out to Skip.

"Let's go. I'll think of something," she assures Unan. They both run out to him, kneeling by his side. "Kermie!" Princess of Havok yells. "Toss me your ice water!" He throws it, and Unan catches it, tossing it over to her. She pulls the top off and begins to pour water into it. "I'll make sure he stays cooled off, and you can ice his leg," she explains, handing the bottle to Unan. Unan feels almost hopeless, but takes the bottle anyway.

"Okay." She rolls it against his leg, which she almost can't bear to look at. Princess of Havok dips her fingers into the water, letting it drop along Skip's forehead. She takes more and smears it on his cheeks, reddened by the sun. It's hard to tell where sweat ends and water droplets begin, but Princess of Havok doesn't seem to care too much, just trying to keep him cool and calm. Unan notices how gentle she tries to be, never letting the water get into his eyes. Unan smiles, despite the depressing situation.

"Are you alright, Skip?" Princess of Havok asks, her voice higher than usual. He says nothing; they can't have any clue how much pain he's in

8

because he won't respond or show any sign of emotion. "Everything's gonna be okay. The ambulance is coming soon," she assures him, pushing his hair away from his face. Unan remembers what the people had been saying. She wonders why they had to be so rude and mimics the gentleness that Princess of Havok uses to keep him unafraid. They begin to hear the wailing of a siren coming closer and closer. It seems like hours. Finally, the ambulance drives up onto the field where they are sitting. The paramedics pull the stretcher out, roughly. Skip can hear them, and his eyes open wide.

"Shit, no," he mutters, moving his head back and forth. Princess of Havok tries to quiet him but can't.

"Ssh, it's okay."

"No, it's not," he replies. He's sweating again, so she places the last drops of water on his warm face.

"Okay, you girls are gonna have to move out of the way," one of the men says. They obey, standing up and backing away, only a couple feet. The paramedics hoist him onto the stretcher, carelessly.

"Thanks, guys," he calls out.

"Bye, Skip."

"Be careful!!!" Unan yells at the paramedics. They make sure the stretcher is on the back of the ambulance, then push it and let it go until it slams against the wall. Skip groans in agony. "Can't you give him some sedatives or something?"

"He doesn't need any. He's a big boy, not a baby," Princess of Havok looks at Unan, sadly.

"There's something wrong with this. How can they be treating him so terribly?" she asks. Unan shrugs.

"I don't know, but I agree with you. It's horrible," Unan replies. Princess of Havok decides to bother them and walks up to the back doors of the ambulance.

"We want to ride in the ambulance and make sure he gets to the hospital," she insists. The man shakes his head.

"No can do. Are you immediate family?"

"No, but..."

"Are you friends of the family?"

"Well, no. But---"

"Then I suggest you little *freaks* get the hell away from this vehicle." The last statement stings, biting its way into Unan's memory. She never forgets statements that hurt; so many, that her mind begins to fill up and sometimes it's hard to concentrate on things.

"Authority sucks. His mom isn't even here!!!" Princess of Havok yells.

"She'll be notified," the man growls back. He scurries into the ambulance and begins to drive away. They both run after it.

"Stop! You can't get away with this!!!"

"Damn you!" Unan cries, loudly, shaking her fist in the air. Eventually, they give up. If only Unan had a flame-throwing banana, none of this would have happened...

The game continues and finally comes to an end. By now, Unan is saddened by the whole event.

"We need to do something fun," she says. Princess of Havok undoes one button on her white blouse.

"I might have an idea," she replies. She starts toward the other side of the field, where the soccer team was.

"Wait a second. Let's go mess with *their* heads," Unan suggests, pointing at the opposing team. Princess of Havok nods, a mischievous smile spreading across her face.

"You know, I like the way you think," she replies, pulling a button off of her shirt. Unan's eyes open wide.

"Now, don't get carried away, Havok. I just meant to screw around with them. Mess with their minds..."

"I know, I know. I'll be careful," she assures Unan. They cross the field, slowly sauntering up to a group of guys standing around, talking.

"Hey, there," Princess of Havok greets them. There are some whistles, and one even dares to walk right up to her and check her out.

"So *that's* how they grow them in Canton, huh?" he asks. The other guys

10

laugh. Unan simply hopes her faithful sidekick won't get herself into trouble.

"Hell yeah," Unan chimes in.

"Well, I thought I saw you girls cheering for the other team. And helping that fatass on the field," he announces, looking at his teammates. Princess of Havok places her hands on her hips.

"Anything for fun. Anything to make the guys feel good," she replies. Unan loves her use of words, but she quickly remembers that she needs to make sure Princess of Havok doesn't do anything stupid, something she'd regret. She'd made a promise to herself, when they first met, that she'd try and take care of this peculiar girl – though she was strange herself.

"Now that's the kind of girl I like." She stands there, allowing him to continue his staring. Before she gets a chance to give a catch phrase or walk away and leave them drooling, he continues talking. "There's just one problem," he adds.

"And what might *that* be?" she asks, figuring the game is still on, and she's the one in control.

"You're an ugly whore!!!" he yells. They all start laughing, taunting her. A stab in the chest; pain courses within and without. She clenches her fist, holding it in front of her stomach. It was an unexpected blow. Unan is confused as to what to do; the word had never caused Princess of Havok such a problem before. She dismissed it as silly, just plain ignorant. Yet now it was the worst thing in the world.

"Havok?" she calls, only hearing heavy breathing. She still stands, unmoving. Anger makes her want to rip someone's vocal chords from their throat. Pain makes her forget. Another phrase tears its way into Unan's memory.

"I'm here. I'm... here." She makes her way to Unan. To be different, the best thing in the world. To be ugly? Mixed feelings. Is that what Alexey and Dave saw? She swore she'd never care about such superficial ideas and materialistic ways. Was it human nature? So maybe it *was* a war, and a mean one at that. It manipulates, lies, cheats. But the fight isn't over; at least, not yet. So many more battles to be won.

"You're not. You'll never be ugly." She places a hand on Princess of Havok's shoulder. "You know that."

"Thanks. But I thought you said you love *all* human beings because they are beautiful," Princess of Havok protests, pausing. A breeze makes its way past.

"Not *all*. Pretty on the inside. *Only* those that are pretty on the inside."

And so, after embracing, the two warriors walk away with a memory never to be forgotten. The sun continues to shine, and the war goes on.

| The Tic-Tac Box

Unan feels there is something wrong when Princess of Havok walks into school. Instead of the usual outfit, she is wearing cargo pants and an army shirt. She still has her combat boots on, though.

"This means war!" she yells to Unan. "I know I said I'm against it, but maybe I changed my mind." Unan smiles, readjusting her Suicide Machines work shirt. She's proud of it because it displays the name "Bob" on the front.

"What's wrong?" she asks.

"They're gonna tear down the school radio tower so they can put in some sports shit!" she replies, flailing her arms. "I'm protesting! Otherwise, Alexey's show will be no more." Unan frowns, furrowing her eyebrows.

"That sucks," is all she can say. Alexey has a radio show; he likes to play Tori Amos, Nine Inch Nails, Bjork, Marilyn Manson, Fiona Apple, Operation Ivy, Tool, and a bunch of other bands. He usually took requests, but some idiots decided to keep harassing him about not playing Mase and Tupac and other things.

"I know. Poor sexy Alexey," Princess of Havok replies, sighing. The radio station is the best thing in the whole school, and now they wanted to ruin that. "So where's your banana?" Unan shrugs.

"Ran out. Dave said he'd bring me one," she replies. Princess of Havok thinks about that, smiling. "Wait, don't look at me like that! Don't even tell me you have any ideas."

"Okay, I don't. Are you gonna call for Warped Tour tickets today?"

"Yeah. So don't worry. Today could be a good day after all," Unan assures her, smiling.

It's been two days since the incident with Skip. The two friends are back in History again, but now the discussion is on drugs, past and present. They listen intently, their attention actually grasped by the whole conversation. Heroin is the main drug being talked about.

"Hey, that reminds me... I haven't seen Boo in a while," Princess of Havok comments. Unan nods. Boo goes to a public school, too, just not theirs. Havok has known her since her father died. Her mother is pretty much non-existent – as a mother, anyway – and she doesn't seem to care what Boo does.

"That's right," Unan replies. "Is she still with Laxy-Boy?" Princess of Havok laughs, remembering Boo's boyfriend's stories about eating chocolate laxatives as a child. He spent more than an hour in the bathroom, and when he got out, he couldn't resist eating more because they tasted so much like real chocolate.

"Yeah, I think so. Laxy-Boy," she giggles. "He's so damn cute. I'm jealous. I'll never forget the time he shook his ass for me... wow." Unan smiles, and the teacher gives them a look as if to say that they better be listening because there will be a quiz later. Right before the bell rings, he stops everybody, making sure they hear his announcement.

"Listen up, people. There's gonna be a quiz next time we have class." Unan scratches the top of her head, getting out of her seat.

"I think I'm psychic," she says aloud.

Later on, during programming, the four friends determine how they are going to protest the sports expansion. Dave doesn't have a banana for Unan...

"Da-ave? Where is it?" she asks. He half smiles, like an innocent child.

"Sorry. Forgot it. But I have something else for you!" he cries, pulling a Tic-Tac box out of his pocket. Unan doesn't understand, a little upset about the banana thing. He notices her look of confusion. "I made it customized for you. See, if you open the cap and pull it back, there's a spring that makes it fling forward. And check *this* out. You can fling safety pins with it!" he explains. It is obvious he is proud of himself, but Unan just has to get used to a new weapon of mass destruction. It won't replace her banana, but it will do for now.

"Okay," she replies, smiling. She is a victim to his charm. His good looks tempt her, and his voice is the most comforting, soothing thing she's ever heard.

At the end of school, Alexey, Dave, Unan, and Havok run outside and stand in front of the radio tower. At first, nobody even notices, but eventually, a large group of students begins to gather to see what's going on.

"Why don't you stupid fucks move away from the tower? They're gonna tear it down, no matter what *you* decide to do," a rather large jock says. Hardly anyone pays attention; no one is truly serious about the whole event yet. Princess of Havok is joking around with Alexey, playfully poking a finger against his chest. Unlike any other day, he's not wearing black. He's wearing regular pants and a homemade t-shirt that says I Love Homosexuals. It's very close fitting, somewhat different for him.

"You are *so* hot," she whispers, pushing him with one finger. He grabs her finger, and she squeals quietly.

"You better watch that finger. I just might bite it right off." Dave interrupts them, tapping on Alexey's shoulder.

"Look. This is *not* gonna be good," he comments, pointing at the gathering crowd. Unan looks, too, curious as to why he seemed so serious.

"Holy shit..." she mutters. An even larger group of students has gathered outside, and they realize there are only four of *them* there to protest the sports complex.

"Listen. You abnormal, science-project-gone-wrong *freaks* better move. Especially *you*, you faggot," a guy growls, mainly talking to Alexey. The four friends hold hands, smiling at each other.

"Intimidation coming, and we really gotta say no to them. TAKE WARNING, TAKE WARNING!" Princess of Havok yells, prompting the others to hold up their joined hands. As the majority insults them, they continue to chant certain lyrics to "Take Warning." Unan quietly pulls out her new Tic-Tac box to see how effectively it works. She launches a few safety pins that fly from her aim and hit a nearby prep.

"Ouch! Watch it!" she cries, holding her bare arm. "Look what she did to me!" She whines to her boyfriend, showing him invisible wounds near her shoulder.

"Who did it?" he asks, gruffly. When the girl points, Unan looks away. "Look at me, you fucking whore! You better stop it!" Eventually, a riot breaks out. The crowd mainly goes for Alexey, whom they *know* hosts a radio show that "nobody" likes, plus the fact that he's wearing that particular shirt today. To Unan and Havok, it seems like a mosh pit at first. But later, it gets extremely violent. Princess of Havok blacks out after her head hits the ground, and once the riot is over, Unan sits on the pavement. Her side aches, and she needs to pull the tip of a safety pin from her leg. Dave has gone, strangely enough, to the authorities. The friends have fallen...

Nobody asks what happened when Unan changes from her cargo pants – which have a small bloodstain now – into her plaid pants. She's back in the coffeehouse, with her parents living in the house behind it like always. She has never cared much for them, but still gets a bit of an allowance slid under her door or slipped into her bags of clothes, which she takes to the laundromat every so often. They never got along, so they figure it's better not to see each other at all. They own the coffeehouse, but Unan rarely ever sees them.

Dave is over, and he has quite a few cuts on his face and arms. Unan is looking for peroxide in the back room where her clothes are. The best she can find is alcohol prep packets, so she brings about ten out to him.

"You know, you're a real darling to do this for me. I'm sure my parents would freak out if they saw me like this. Wait... they always freak out when I'm around," he says, thinking about it for a moment. Unan opens a package and pulls out the alcohol pad, rubbing it lightly against a cut on his cheek. He takes in a sharp breath. The cut is deep.

"What, did they cut you with a broken bottle or something? Shit," Unan mutters, shaking her head.

"I think they slashed at me with anything and everything possible," he replies, looking down at his hands. "I hope Alex and Havok are alright." Unan stops to rub her eye, which seems to have an eyelash stuck on it.

"Yeah. Are we going to the hospital today?"

"If you want to. You know, I think I have a cut underneath my shirt. There was a tear in the front when I checked..." he starts, beginning to take off his shirt. Unan clutches the next alcohol packet, hoping that she doesn't die because then, she wouldn't be able to help him anymore. She takes a deep breath.

"I can take care of that for you," she replies, gladly offering. The gash is near his stomach, so she needs to squat down a little, holding his back with one hand for support. His back is slightly damp from the earlier struggle with the crowd. Dave isn't realizing just how much fun Unan is having, but it makes her sad to see how many times he was cut. She could only wonder how Alexey felt right now...

When Unan and Dave arrive at the hospital, Princess of Havok is laying – on her side – next to Alexey, who looks like he's sleeping.

"How bad is it?" Dave asks, walking over to a cushioned chair. Unan makes her way over to Princess of Havok. She turns over and looks at them with red eyes.

"Wow. Laying here, I keep thinking this is all a dream, and I've yet to wake up. You guys proved me wrong," she says, forcing a tiny smile. "There was minor internal bleeding at first, but he's gonna be fine. They

17

took care of it." Unan breathes a sigh of relief and puts a hand to Princess of Havok's forehead. She smiles and places her own hand over Unan's. "It's okay, conqueror. I'm gonna be alright, too."

"You know, you guys are like Xena and Gabrielle," Dave comments. They giggle; a nervous laugh.

"Except I don't really get to battle people, like with a sword or anything. And I prefer not to wear extremely tight leather bondage outfits," Unan replies, a million thoughts zooming through her mind. She pictures herself in a Xena outfit; no, she makes a few changes. There, that's about right. She soon remembers where she is and clears her mind again. Princess of Havok has begun to doodle on the bed sheets with a pen:

Sexey Alexey wuz here

"You little punk rocker. Destroying hospital property..." Dave starts, smiling. Princess of Havok moves again but does not get off the bed. The room is dimly lit, so Unan doesn't even realize until now that she has a black eye. She feels sorry for Princess of Havok but says nothing about it. Alexey finally wakes up; he is bruised and beaten, cut and broken.

"Hey, guys," he says. He notices Princess of Havok right next to him. "Whoa, close-up shot." He attempts to laugh, but stops.

"Oh yeah, he has a couple fractured ribs," Princess of Havok explains. "I forgot to mention that."

They talk about what happened for a while, and then decide to let Alexey rest. Princess of Havok offers to stay, and neither Dave nor Unan argue. They figure she will probably feel better, knowing exactly how Alexey is doing. By the time they leave, she has fallen sleep with one hand on his chest and her head on his shoulder. They look like a painting.

They return to the coffeehouse in time to catch some crappy acts, including some chick from their school. She's wearing a white baby tee with a light sweater – also white – and jeans that could use a lot more material. She also has saddle shoes on. Unan and Dave sit at a booth, and Dave throws a spoon towards the small "stage."

"Singin' about peace... where were you for the riot?!" he yells, obviously enjoying himself.

"Yeah, ya dizzy bitch!" The girl squeals and frantically picks up her guitar, heading for one side of the stage. The spoon clatters against the seat she was using, then drops and slides across the wood floor, landing at her small feet. She treads over to the nearest couch to cry on her boyfriend's shoulder. Unan and Dave smile at each other over the tabletop.

Later on, when the crowds are gone, the two friends sit, talking.

"So, what are *your* parents' pet peeves?" Unan asks him. "I mean, do they not like you for a certain reason?"

"Well... I'm not sure. But it doesn't matter because I hate them just the same. Pricks. Always talking about what they believe in and stand for, but they can't even explain why they do."

"Yeah, me and my parents *never* got along. I think I was an accident. Seriously! But I do better by myself. They're never around anyway. Well, they leave me money. But that's different from actually being around," she explains. She begins to wonder what it would be like if all she did was what her parents told her, and she never learned to think for herself. She would probably be wearing a cute little sundress with white sandal shoes because that was what you were *supposed* to wear. The kind of girl who constantly pined for every guy's attention. They were talked about and had a fuss made over them. Unan does not understand why people can't love her for who she is, but then she remembers whom she is with. She pulls the Tic-Tac box out of her pocket and rubs the plastic sides, creating warmth yet being careful not to crack it; she appreciates her special present from Dave. He looked so happy and proud of himself when he'd given it to her. Besides, there was always time to buy more bananas.

"I know what you mean," he replies. Unan still can't believe she's seen his chest. To her, that's a big deal. Not only did she see his chest, but she also touched his stomach. Quite an accomplishment for one day.

"Sorry to change the subject, but can I see your cut again? You know, the one on your stomach. I just want to make sure I cleaned it good enough, and it's not getting infected or anything," Unan says, making up an excuse.

19

"You sure you want to see it?"

"Yeah. Trust me, I'm an expert when it comes to things like this." He lifts his shirt over his head and pulls it off his arms. Unan takes a deep breath and almost forgets to let it out. She thinks of all the guys she's ever seen without shirts; none of them in person, until today. Well, only at concerts, but that didn't count because she couldn't touch them. Billie Joe Armstrong, that cute little Tom DeLonge from Blink 182, Tim Armstrong... maybe even Laxy-Boy a couple times, but he was just too damn skinny and self-mutilated. Dave was something else.

"Does it look okay?"

"Actually, it *does* look better than it did before," Unan answers, truthfully. She tries not to be school-girlish about the whole predicament.

"Really? Cool. I think I'll just leave my shirt off. It's kinda warm in here," Dave says, throwing it to the side. That catches her by surprise, and she grabs the end of the table with her hand.

"Well, it's not that warm. I mean, we could always open a window," she replies, quickly. Unan realizes that it sounds a little suspicious.

"If I didn't know any better, I'd think you didn't want me to keep it off. That's alright. I can always put it back on..." Dave suggests.

"No! I mean, yes! No! I don't know!" She slowly begins to lose control of her own mind.

"What's the matter?" Unan tries to think what Princess of Havok would say at a time like this.

"If you keep it off, I may have to jump on you," she replies, smiling. Wow, that came out better than she expected. Thoughts whizzed through her brain. Alexey had a nickname, Sexy Alexey, and now Dave needed one. She thought to herself, naughtily, Delicious Dave? She bit her lip, trying not to laugh out loud.

"Well, if you really feel the urge, go ahead." Good old sensual Dave. She actually may have, if she didn't feel so scared and nervous about it.

"Don't say that."

"Seriously. Go ahead."

"No, really. You don't want to say that," Unan replies.

"If I didn't, then I wouldn't say it. I don't mind. You're good company, so what's wrong with having a little fun?" he offers, smiling. She really has a tough time restraining herself, but the poor boy is in pain. He *must* be, with all those cuts and bruises... but he's so... tempting. His eyes are blue, shining like headlights in the dead of night, his hair midnight black. He licks his lips once, his tongue seeming to move in slow motion.

"Let's just talk. I don't want to start anything I can't finish," Unan replies, heading over to the couch. Dave follows along like a little child.

"Can we at least sit together?" he asks. She nods and yawns, putting a hand over her mouth. He sits down at one end of the sofa, cross-legged, facing the other side. She plops down in front of him and leans back. He puts his arms around her, and she hangs onto them.

"Hope you don't mind, but I decided I'm staying here tonight," he announces.

"Fine by me. At least I'm not alone." They listen as a car, pumping bass, flies down the street. Dave is breathing softly, and Unan attempts to get her heart to beat at the same time his does. As they are silent, Unan accomplishes the feat. For a moment, two lives are completely in sync with each other. She feels she could die right now and still be happy.

"You should never be alone. Nobody should *ever* have to be alone," Dave says, quietly. The words come from out of nowhere, yet they seem to make the most sense at this time. He kisses the top of her head, lightly, and she falls asleep, hoping the next day will never come.

Unfortunately, the next day dawns, yet quietly enough that Unan doesn't seem to mind. As she rolls over to get more comfortable, she falls off the couch. She gives a muffled cry and lifts her head from the floor.

"You okay?" Dave asks, half-laughing. She nods and pushes herself up with her arms. He points to a bowl on one of the tables with a shaky finger. "Bananas were on sale at the store."

"Jesus! What time do you get up in the morning, anyway?" Unan asks, clumsily walking over to a booth.

21

"Whenever. This morning it just happened to be a bit early. *Someone* was snoring pretty loudly..."

"Me? Really?"

"No." It seems like a trivial, silly joke, but they both laugh. "I just wanted to make sure I got your banana."

After visiting the hospital a second time, they bring Princess of Havok back with them. They have to walk by a park on the way back to the coffeehouse. Many people from the previous day's riot were congregated on the grass.

"The fuckers have probably been following us. Damn half-wits," Dave mutters. He walks in front of Unan and Havok, as if to protect them from some impending danger. A few jocks head over to the three friends.

"I'm surprised you still want to show your faces in public after what happened yesterday. You guys better be careful."

"Is that *all* you can say?!! If I had a dollar for every time I've heard somebody say that this week... poor Alexey," Princess of Havok moans, changing her tone. She looks to Dave for some sign of support. He simply stands his ground.

"*You* pricks better watch it. We didn't ask for any trouble. Our friend is already in the hospital," Dave says, squeezing his hands into fists.

"Oh, that gay pride faggot, right?"

"*Fuck you*!!!" Princess of Havok yells, trying to break past Dave. He holds onto her, keeping her behind him.

"Whoa, check it out! It's that whore from school. Hey, slut! What's the matter? Daddy been showin' you who's boss?" a rapper cries, loudly.

"Excuse me?" Havok says, cupping a hand over her black eye. "I don't think *you're* in any position to say something like that." She stands with her legs apart and her hands on her hips; it's quite comical, even though it's her usual stance, because she seems more like a cartoon character than a real person.

"Huh?" the guy replies.

"Oh yeah, you know what I mean. You have no right to say that when you'd come to me if your girlfriend wasn't putting out," she explains, with a flair only the Princess of Havok could muster up at a time like this. His eyes open wide, and she simply smiles, knowing what his stupid girlfriend is going to say before she says it.

"Justin? Would you really do that, baby?" she asks, airheadedly. He brushes the question off, lightly. Unan jumps up onto a park bench, pumping her fist into the air, waving her banana.

"Face it, you good-for-nothing asswipes! You may knock us down, but you're never gonna walk on us! We'll fucking be heard, whether you care or not! Power to the people!!!" she yells, delivering her short speech. Dave begins to sing softly...

"Heard all that shit before, about stomping out any difference. We say stand together. Not to fight... just to exist..." Operation Ivy lyrics once again, just like before the riot. Maybe a sign of deja vu, but nobody realizes that. As things slowly progress, the friends find themselves against a crowd once again. Dave doesn't let Unan and Princess of Havok fight, though. He holds a rock high above his head and threatens to smash anyone who comes near them. Eventually, things die down. They receive a message that school officials want to see them in a couple days about the protest on Friday. Unan and Princess of Havok, for the first time, cry in each other's arms. Dave sits on the curb, head in hands, looking absolutely dejected. Worried for Alex and disappointed that it's come to this again. Passers-by gawk at the weary friends until Dave scares them off with Unan's ever-present Tic-Tac box. It couldn't be a jinx, could it? After all, Dave had created it and given it to Unan.

Confusion sets in once again. They don't cry because they are wanted by school authorities; they feel guilty. At one time, war seemed as though it could never affect them, but all of a sudden there's a new meaning to the word. Those that thought they were against it are now a very large part of it. And someone has suffered because of it...

Yet another memory never to be forgotten. The sun continues to shine, and the war goes on.

| Happiness and Judgment

Unan describes her experience with Dave to Princess of Havok. Her eyes remain open wide throughout the whole story, except for the one that's black. It's more open than usual; the eyelid is a quarter of the way up.

They are bumming around the local park for the crummy annual festival. But this year's isn't too bad. There are still the usual airheaded people who are complimenting each other while wearing the same exact outfits. The ever-present couples wander everywhere, seeming to taunt. Yet this year, it seems as though the festival is actually an escape from the recent tragedies they've faced.

Instead of walking around, they choose a grassy spot on a hill to set their butts down and ponder about life. After describing Delicious Dave events, Unan stands at the top of the hill with her arms outstretched.

"I'm gonna roll down," she announces. She wraps her arms around herself and begins to roll. Her blue, spiky hair seems to dance just a few inches from the ground. Her mind thinks back to when she was younger and how her pants would practically be on backwards by the time she stopped rolling. But now a bondage ring belt prevents her plaid pants from going anywhere. Things have changed so much since she was five, so young and innocent. Pure. She swipes a hand across her sweat-beaded forehead and remembers the time when she and Princess of Havok drove away with a refrigerated truck. They were thirteen or fourteen, and they happened to spot a man rushing out of the cab of a truck. He ran into the supermarket across the street and left it running.

******

"Check it out. That guy just left a refrigerated chicken truck running with the keys in the ignition," Unan says. Princess of Havok saunters over to the back of the truck. She climbs up and yanks on the door, causing it to slide up about a foot.

"Hmm. Chicken, chicken... whoa! There's about three whole cases of Surge!!!" she yells, jumping up and down.

"Seems a bit misplaced. I wonder how that happened," Unan replies, pondering and leaning against the truck.

"I don't care how it happened, just give *me* a hit!" Unan wanders over to the cab and peers into the window.

"Get in. Let's go."

And so they go. As they speed down a few side streets, Unan takes down ten mailboxes, three flower gardens, and one stop sign. Some people sitting out on their porches gawk and point at the refrigerated truck flying down the street. As they head toward the freeway, Princess of Havok becomes fidgety.

"Do you know what you're doing?!!" she cries.

"Hell yeah! You know how many times I've driven a go-kart?" Unan replies. Just before the ramp to the expressway, she pulls the truck over onto the grass and turns it off. Princess of Havok breathes a sigh of relief and looks at her questioningly. "You didn't think I was gonna take this baby on the freeway, did you?" They both smile at each other and hop out of the cab.

Once they've had all three cases of Surge and have nearly pissed themselves afterwards, the authorities find them. A cop car pulls up next to the refrigerated truck Unan and Princess of Havok have stolen.

"Hey!"

******

"Hey!" Princess of Havok yells. "Did you fucking die down there or something?" Unan's mind snaps back to reality. She looks up at the disgustingly bright, blue sky.

"No, I'm still alive... whether that's good or bad," she replies, simply. Unan rolls over and sees that they've put in a new playground. The kid in her takes over, and she runs to the slide, climbing up the ladder. Princess of Havok sits up to get a better look at what her friend is doing. As Unan begins to slide down, she smiles.

"Whee!" Her cry stops short as her body slows. She is unmoving, barely even halfway down the slide. "Dammit!" she yells, banging the metal sides. A few children stare, and then run past, their mother rushing them along, telling them not to stare. Unan thinks about what a shame it is that the mother is afraid of *them*, but would probably let her children play in the street. She finally has an idea. She pulls her legs up, and as she curls up into the fetal position, she feels her body continue its journey down the slide. She goes right over and end and lands on the ground with a thump.

"Let's go check out the action on the other side of the park," Princess of Havok suggests. Unan stands up, wiping dirt from her pants. She realizes that they've moved half an inch over to the side. Maybe her childhood isn't over after all.

They begin to walk to the other side of the park, stopping at a small bridge to take pictures. Unan takes a picture of Princess of Havok looking sad and disappointed – which she later hangs in Alexey's hospital room. Princess of Havok takes a picture of Unan standing on the railing, gazing into the distance, looking very punk rock. After the picture is taken, the sun makes its way to a spot just above them, shining against Unan's blue hair. She continues looking into the woods and does not jump from her perch on the railing. Instead, she sits down on it, careful not to fall over the side. Princess of Havok tries to spot what is so interesting, hoping her friend will start talking again and tell her what it is. Unan doesn't open her mouth.

"Unan? You alright?" she asks, stealing her from her trance.

"Yeah. Um, well, let's go," she says, jumping off the railing. They continue walking.

Once they get to the other side, they find that there isn't a whole lot of action for them to join in on. The paddleboat rides are about to close, neither of them have money for cotton candy, and there's not much to look at in terms of people. Unan suggests they sit down in a shady spot because the sun is getting to be too much. They plop down and make themselves at home, just as some cheesy music starts playing at the amphitheater. It eventually gets to them, though.

"I wish sexy Alexey was here. I hope he's doing okay," Princess of Havok sighs, picking at her battered, old, checkered wingtips. Their small audiocassette player is blaring Rancid from its tiny speaker. People give them dirty looks as they walk by, but neither of them pays any attention at all. Princess of Havok lays back, grass clinging to her large-in-the-crotch dress pants. She straightens her short-sleeved polyester shirt; her collar is still messed up and uneven.

"Yeah, I..." Unan starts. There is a rustling behind them; a guy steps out from the side of the trees. His face is clearly computer generated or airbrushed. No human could look this perfect and yet, be standing right in front of them. It's one of those moments like on TV when everything slows down, something seems to click, it's confusing and at the same time makes the most absolutely perfect sense. He appears to be staring at Unan, not watching where he's going.

"Hi," he says, slightly nodding his head. Princess of Havok doesn't speak, her mouth dry from hanging open. She hears an "uhhh" sound escaping from Unan's lips.

"Uhhh... uhhh... hi-ee," Unan replies, enunciating her greeting. The guy smiles and continues walking, his hands in his pockets so that his shirt is pulled almost high enough to show the butt of his jeans. "Ohhh... wow. Oh my God." Princess of Havok starts gathering their stuff together and stands up with a gleam in her eye. "Where are you going?"

"We're gonna follow that guy, dammit, or my name's not Princess of Havok!" she answers, holding the tape player into the air. Unan stands up, too, flicking a spider from her shoulder.

"You're right. We *should* follow him," she says. For some reason, the day is making her weary. It's taking too long to pass, and she doesn't feel right. Her limbs are weak, and she has to drag herself to follow Princess of Havok. Things are a blur, and she can't remember what she's done today.

As they follow him, he looks back twice. They both dodge back and forth behind vendors' trailers. The guy is eating a popsicle – "How sensual. Look at that tongue!" Princess of Havok comments – and smiling to himself. They suspect he probably knows they're stalking him. Finally, he decides to end the game by stopping in an arts and crafts tent. While he stares at a painting, Unan stares at him. Eventually, tired of waiting for action, Princess of Havok pushes her toward him, and her limp body stops just inches away from his back. His butt looks quite tempting, calling out to her. "Grab me! Come here and grab me..." He is slightly bent over. Unan feels a bit more awake, but only for a moment, reaching her hand out toward him. Just before she touches it, he spins around, and she pulls her hand back quickly.

"Hi there," he says, not seeming upset at all. Instead, he continues smiling. Unan becomes confused, not understanding his strange behavior. It's as if he *wanted* her to touch him, as if he was waiting as anxiously for that moment as she was.

"Hey. Um, I'm Unan. You walked by us over at the lake, and well, you looked sort of interesting. I thought maybe I should introduce myself," she explains with ease. The words aren't hers, and neither is the behavior. Princess of Havok stands behind her, looking on in surprise and awe.

"You're kidding, right? Me, interesting?" he asks, glancing down at himself. "I look like every other guy in this damn town. Now you and your friend, to tell you the truth, caught my attention. You seem very intriguing.

29

Oh, my name's Ryan Thomas, by the way," he announces. Unan is obviously infatuated with this stranger.

"Yeah, nice to meet you. Well, would you like to stay for the fireworks with us? We'll be here until eleven or so." Unan crosses her fingers behind her back.

"Sure, I'd love to. But I need to go grab a drink first. So I'll meet you back where you were. Right off the lake is a good spot to catch the lights," he says, walking off in the other direction.

"Okay! See you there!" Unan calls out, waving. She receives a dirty look from Princess of Havok, who is still standing just behind her. "What?"

"I thought we weren't staying that late."

"We are now."

Ryan later joins them by the makeshift lake in the park. He and Unan talk to no end, going on and on while the sky gets darker and darker. They share an iced tea. Ryan "accidentally" got two straws instead of three, so Princess of Havok offers to give up her share of the drink. She watches as they tell each other's life stories. There's got to be something wrong; perhaps Unan has eaten some tainted brownies, but she doesn't recall her having eaten anything at all today. How could Unan have totally forgotten about Dave and joined up with some guy she'd just met. Sure he was... perfect? But he was perfect in *looks*, and that's all they could tell from what they knew so far. It wasn't like Unan to be so open with someone.

Dark sets in, and Princess of Havok notices them sitting closer together. At first, she writes it off as her imagination and nothing else. Once the fireworks start, she tries to concentrate on them instead of Unan and Ryan. She feels... jealous? No, not jealous. Left out. She can no longer hear their conversation. Jokingly, she turns around to pretend like she thought they left her. But when she turns around, she finds them kissing. Not just kissing, but *kissing*. They don't seem to realize that she's watching them intently, not understanding the whole situation. If only it were a dream and she could pinch herself to wake up. In an attempt to console herself, she grabs a safety pin from her shoelace and stabs the tip of her finger. Blood slowly begins to ooze out, dark red, and she realizes that it's not a dream. They're really going at it now, right here on the grass.

"Unan, I just remembered I have to... to do something... at home. Yeah, so I'll see you tomorrow," Princess of Havok says, loudly, above the crack of the fireworks. They slow down long enough for Unan to nod and let her know she's been heard. Then, they go right back at it. Princess of Havok walks away, almost disgusted. How could she do this to Dave when he cared so much about her? Of course, he'd probably never said anything – to Unan – in particular about his feelings for her. He didn't want to move too quickly, afraid that she'd already been through enough. Now he might not even get this chance. The least she can do to make herself feel better is to terrorize people with her music. As she walks away, Falling Sickness blares out of the tape player, and she holds it out near the back of people's heads. If someone's going to suffer because of her anger, it might as well be them.

Unan wakes up the next morning on the couch again, under an old sheet she's been using since she started living in the coffeehouse. It's just a normal morning, right? No, there's something wrong. She's wearing only boxers and a bra. It wasn't *that* warm last night. Yet her forehead is beaded with sweat. And Unan finally remembers what happened. She feels sick to her stomach. She looks around, wondering if she's alone. She stands up, wrapping the damp sheet around her. From the bathroom in the back, she hears the toilet flush and the faucet turn on for about two minutes. After the noise stops, Ryan walks out wearing only boxers.

"Hey," he greets her. He looks so good to Unan that she almost forgets what she is going to do. It's hard to remember anything with this pounding headache.

"Get out," she says, simply. She can't look at him, knowing what they've done, knowing what *he's* done to her.

"What?"

"I said get out." He pulls on his pants and throws on his shirt, beginning to button it. As he sits down and puts his shoes on, he gets angry.

"I don't believe this. You know you liked it. In fact, *I* happen to know you *loved* it because you were screaming for more."

"*Just get the fuck out!!!*" she yells, hurting her own head. She grasps it with both hands and begins to cry. Unan would throw up and get the sick feeling out of her stomach, but she has nothing in her to let out.

"Fine, dammit! I don't know why, all of a sudden, you have a problem with this. But one thing I *do* know is that people are gonna hear about it!" Ryan yells back, heading for the door.

"I don't even know you," Unan sobs, quietly. "How could you do this, you *asshole*?!!" He slams the door, and she flings the sheet at it, feeling weaker than ever. She slides off the booth seat and crumples into a heap on the floor.

Meanwhile, Princess of Havok gets up to the sun shining in her bedroom window. She wonders if Unan is over her "fling." Perhaps she was just feeling sexually frustrated or her hormones were raging in overdrive; maybe the guy was just too damn perfect, but there was no such thing, was there? Maybe it was the fact that he was *there*, available, interested? Unan was given the perfect opportunity to jump his bones, and, well... the rest was history. Princess of Havok dresses quickly and walks to the coffeehouse. Luckily, for Unan, it's not open yet. She picks her head up from off the floor just as Princess of Havok steps in.

"So, is it out of your system yet?" she asks, smiling. She has no clue as to what went on last night. Unan gives her a questioning look. She was afraid that Ryan might be coming back again to mess with her. Lay his charm on her once again so that she might let him have his way.

"Huh?"

"You know what I mean. Didja let him pop your cherry?" Havok asks, playfully. Unan sighs and lets her head fall back to the floor. "Cuz if that's what you wanted, maybe we should celebrate now..."

"Yes! Okay, I let him fuck me. God, I can't believe I let him. And why are you talking to me like that anyway? Are you jealous?" Unan replies, not thinking before she speaks.

"Hell no!!! What, you get broken in and all of a sudden you're better than

32

me?" Princess of Havok answers, feeling a bit disappointed. Is she losing the conqueror to another side?

"I never said that. And a mother is not exactly what I need right now," Unan declares, trying her best to get up without stumbling. She almost looks drunk or like she's just coming down from a high.

"I'm not trying to be a mother," Princess of Havok states, dejectedly. She looks down at the floor, wishing everything will just go away, but she knows better. "I felt hurt yesterday. Partly because you just started talking to that *Ryan* guy. But mostly because you felt comfortable telling a stranger your life story and letting him deflower you afterwards! How could you do that? I'm not acting like a mother," she repeats. "I was trying to look after you." Unan stands by the couch, holding onto it for support. She looks at Princess of Havok with a blank stare, seeing her black eye and the sad expression on her face. For a brief moment, she wonders why she wasn't really hurt during either of the fights that broke out, but realizes she *was* hurt in a totally different way. Unan collapses onto the sofa, allowing herself to be enveloped into the cushions. Princess of Havok runs over, unsure if she is okay or not. Unan feels the way Renton must have in *Trainspotting* when he OD'd on heroin and sank into the carpet. "You alright, Unan?"

"Yeah." Something wet falls onto her cheek as Princess of Havok plops down next to her, and Unan props her head against her shoulder. A light flow of tears begins to rain from her already-red eyes.

"No, you're not! You're crying, Unan. Don't cry," Princess of Havok protests, wrapping her arms around Unan's head and matting down her hair in an attempt to soothe her.

"I didn't mean to be so rude. I feel like... I don't know what I feel like! I wasn't thinking last night. I'm still not thinking clearly now, and..." Unan rambles, shaking her head and closing her eyes tightly. It hurts to think, to speak, to move.

"It's okay. Just stop crying, and we'll get you all cleaned up," Princess of Havok assures her. She notices Unan still shaking. "What's the matter?"

"My head... it's killing me. It's worse than a damn hangover," she tries to explain. Havok lays a hand, lightly, on her shoulder.

"Oh, Unan, you didn't even eat anything yesterday, did you?" She doesn't respond. "Did you take anything for your headache?"

"I downed a couple Extra Strength Tylenol in the morning and then some Advil later on."

"No wonder you weren't thinking straight. Taking those extra strength things is like being high!" She pauses for a moment. "Oh, shit!!! Damn, damn, damn! We're completely screwed! I guess we both forgot what today is," she says, quieting down. She is answered by a confused look from Unan. "We have to explain the protest to the school officials today."

"Oh, God. When is it?"

"This afternoon. You think we can get you fixed up?"

"Yeah." She gets up to change but stops before she reaches the back room. "Havok? Thanks for coming over. I think what I needed was to be straightened out. That guy, Ryan..." She rephrases her sentence. "It might be hard to trust people again."

"You can't trust anybody, anyway. But don't worry. I'm here. I'll help you."

And so, for once, the sidekick takes care of the conqueror. Unan changes, throwing on a Rancid shirt and some brown pants with white stripes down the side. Princess of Havok attempts to cook a breakfast of eggs, bacon, and toast. Once Unan comes out from the back room, they both decide that a little music is needed. But when the tape player is turned on, Goldfinger is the first thing they hear:

How much do you want?
And how far can I take you?
How bad does this hurt?
And how much do I want you?

Princess of Havok quickly shakes her head and stops the tape. It was always their favorite part of the song, but perhaps this isn't the best timing for it. Instead, she pops in Hole and then Pinhead Gunpowder. Eventually, the coffeehouse begins to fill up with people; the regulars, who know that it

34

opens around eleven or whenever the workers decide to show up in the morning. As the people go through their daily routine, the two friends continue to talk and laugh, forgetting about last night's incident. By now, Stone Temple Pilots are on, requested by a girl that came there every day to sit around and do nothing. They wait for Dave to arrive so they can go to the meeting. As Unan turns to see who just walked in the door, she sees Ryan sitting with a blond girl from school. Their eyes meet for a split-second, and he excuses himself from the table, heading over to theirs.

"Could I talk to you for a second? In private," he adds, glaring at Princess of Havok. She looks at him in awe.

"Funny you should notice me. I'm sure you could just ignore me and pretend I'm not here, which you were very capable of doing last night," she replies, smiling. She makes no attempt to move from her seat.

"Alright. Well, anyway," he says, turning back to Unan. "I just wanted to say I'm sorry about everything. I realize we probably should've taken it slower."

"Just stop right there. This is all bullshit. *You* don't even believe one word you're saying, you hypocrite!" Unan cries.

"Why don't you believe me?"

"You're an asshole. A jerk. I should've seen it earlier, but I was too stupid and drugged to know right from wrong. You walk around with your head up your own ass like you're God's gift to women. So what are you gonna do with the airhead over there? Screw her tonight and write her name down on the list of virgins you've popped? You know, girls aren't trophies, and you ain't the shit," Unan says. She takes a deep breath as he looks at her in wonder and amazement.

"Don't talk about her like that. She's my girlfriend," he replies, then realizes he's just ruined his own game. Unan shakes her head in disgust.

"You are one ugly, perverted pig of a guy!" she yells. "God, I can't believe I did it with you," Unan says, incredulously. "Just do me a favor, okay? Don't step foot in this coffeehouse *ever* again!"

"If it makes any difference at all, I think you were *great*," he adds in one

35

last, triumphant statement.

"*You* weren't," she retorts, sitting back down. Ryan takes his "girlfriend" and leaves the coffeehouse. Princess of Havok smiles at her, proud. They both understand that Unan has just done one of the hardest things she may ever have to do in her life. "Well, it's definitely a surprise that I should be broken in before you," Unan says, letting Havok know that she's ready to joke about her experience for now. After all, neither of them can do anything to change what happened.

"Hmm... Unan the deflowered Conqueror and her faithful, prude sidekick, Princess of Havok. Yeah, I think I could get used to that. Eventually," she replies, grinning. Just then, Dave comes in to take them to the meeting.

"Can you do one more thing for me? Please don't tell Dave. Maybe I can start over again. Just totally forget this ever happened and begin the pursuit of a new guy," Unan explains, looking off into the distance.

"I can handle that. And this new guy would be... Dave?"

"Maybe. Do you think he could learn to like me?" Unan asks, a bit self-consciously.

"Well..." Princess of Havok starts. She doesn't want to share her sweet secret with Unan. She wonders if it will be hard to keep from two friends the fact that each one likes the other. It's almost like a soap opera. She figures she will simply let it run its course. An excited Unan interrupts her thoughts.

"Ssh. He's almost here. Let's go," she says. Dave escorts them to the hospital.

The meeting with school authorities is being held in Alexey's hospital room. It's almost a humorous sight; the disciplinary committee dressed in skirts and dress pants, three confused teenagers, and a boy lying in a hospital bed.

"This is a goddamn joke," is the first thing Princess of Havok can say. But once she sees Alexey half-sitting in bed, she can't help but smile. "Sexy Alexey!!!" she cries, running and jumping onto his bed, careful not to hurt him. She looks just like a little kid, pressing a hand to his pale face to see if he's okay. He laughs, clumsily trying to lift himself up a little more. The principal clears her throat.

"Can we please get this started? And get the girl off the bed," she orders in a disgusted tone. Unan and Dave help her off the bed, each of them taking one arm, but not before she can sneak a quick kiss on the forehead.

The meeting mainly consists of pointing fingers and accusations. The friends had hoped that maybe they'd get a chance to tell their side of the story, but it doesn't seem like they will. Dave doesn't understand why everything has to be so corrupt; Unan is confused as to how she can speak without being interrupted or ignored; Princess of Havok is filled with hatred. How can they stand there, seeing Alexey the way he is, and not let him say something? They must feel at least an *ounce* of sympathy, but if they don't, then they must be the stereotypical stone cold, unfeeling authority figures that they're afraid of.

"May the injured speak?" Alexey asks. Everyone turns to look at him. "I, personally, don't know why you insist on blaming us for everything. If we'd started it, we most likely would not be the ones who were hurt. Yet, somehow, we are. Isn't that the least bit suspicious? Yes, we're guilty of speaking out and standing up for what we believe in," he says with the most manners and composure of anyone in the room. He motions for Princess of Havok to come over. She stands next to his bed and lets him rest his hand on her back. "And if we're the violent hoodlums you accuse of starting the riot at school, I'd like to see you explain why none of the people in the crowd were hurt."

"So you're trying to tell me that none of you even fought back? It's impossible. That would be human nature," the vice principal protests.

"Nobody fought. We simply stood our ground and waited for it to end."

"Especially s--- I mean, Alex. He never even moved. I watched him get beaten up," Princess of Havok explains.

"And you didn't do anything?"

"No, someone punched her in the face. Then when she fell to the pavement, she blacked out," Dave says, reaching over to hold Unan's hand. She becomes flustered, not knowing what to do. She doesn't recall anything like this ever happening before.

"And what about you? Were you hurt in any way?" they ask him.

"I got some cuts and gashes I can show you. And *this* baby," he adds, pointing to his cheek, "is from the riot, too." He acts like a proud soldier come home from battle.

"And *you*?" Unan is still in shock from Dave holding her hand.

"Uhhh... well, shit! Of course I got hurt," she blurts out, afraid that she may have just blown their chances at receiving any slack.

"Somebody threw a bottle at her side..." Dave quickly fills in, but is soon interrupted.

"Please refrain from the profanity."

"Sorry. I got a bottle thrown at me and somehow, there was stuff stuck in my leg."

"Alright, this is all cute and everything. I know you're all friends, and you're sticking up for each other. However, we weren't there, and we don't know the truth of the matter. How do we know these aren't self-inflicted wounds? We've seen stranger, and you never know what teenagers will do nowadays. We've decided to deny your request that the radio tower stay up, and the sports building will go in as scheduled," the principal explains. She's very long-winded about it when she may as well have just said "No. We're not letting you get your way, and it'll be a cold day in hell before we believe you."

"Well, if that's how you want to be about it," Princess of Havok replies through gritted teeth. Alexey rubs her back, lightly, and she sits down next to him on the bed.

"Thank you for coming. We'll notify you if our final decision requires any disciplinary action." Dave looks at them in surprise.

"That's just dandy! What do you mean by that?" he asks, demanding that they reveal their master plan. The vice principal opens his mouth, ready to speak, and the principal fidgets wildly.

"We haven't yet spoken to the other side."

"What?!!" Alexey cries. "And you've already made your decision?"

"Yes, we have. Regardless of what anyone has to say, you did *not* follow the proper protocol for a protest on school grounds. And your schoolmates were just acting in response to your unorganized actions. Not to mention when you went to the police, it brought the school some very bad press. Besides, the new sports complex will bring the school more money." The principal herds the committee through the door, trying to stop the vice principal from releasing any more information.

"We'll be in touch!!!" she calls out, nervously. Unan squeezes Dave's hand tightly. He says nothing; the whole room is silent for at least two minutes.

"This is so one-sided. I hate this! Is it always going to be this way? I just wanna... hurt them!" Dave cries, curling his hand into a fist.

"No, now come on. It could be worse. We might not have even been able to get our say. We're lucky we got that. And who can say they got to cry "shit!" in a conversation with the principal?" Alexey asks, smiling. They all laugh, Unan blushing. Dave kisses the top of her head, like a father would kiss his child. "So let's celebrate. I get out of this place in a few days, and school is almost over. What more could we ask for?" Just then, a nurse brings in his dinner. A banana sits atop a sandwich wrapped in wax paper. "See? Things could be looking up."

They are proud of their courageous friend. Yet another memory never to be forgotten, and the war goes on.

| Honesty and a New Addition

A new face begins to appear at the coffeehouse. It belongs to a tall, gaunt boy who always shows up in a black shirt, black shorts, torn black stockings, and black boots. He never talks to anyone; he just sits at a table in the corner and keeps to himself. He appears to be writing or doodling on a notepad that he carries around with him. Princess of Havok is elected to try and get him to talk. She slowly walks over and sits down across from him.

"Hey!" she greets him, cheerfully. He nods and continues writing furiously. She frowns, furrowing her eyebrows. "You new here? I don't remember ever seeing you."

"Yeah, I'm new." He stares off into space, seeming to be thinking about something that's troubling him.

"I'm not bothering you, am I? 'Cause if I am, we could just talk later or something," Princess of Havok offers. She taps her hand on the table to a

Sublime song – "Caress Me Down." Unan is getting many dirty looks from the people who know she's sometimes in charge of the music. But she's too busy watching Delicious Dave eat a banana.

"No, that's okay. I guess I could probably use a break for now." He stretches his lanky legs out, his boots nearly hitting Havok's. "Sorry."

"No problem! So, what's your name?"

"J--- well, you can call me Mortys. That's, um, my pen name," he explains, hesitantly.

"Wow, that's awesome. Do you have stuff published?" she asks, sincerely interested. He folds his hands and rests them on his lap.

"Nothing national. I mean, no books or anything that big. Just a few magazines," he answers, modestly. A girl comes to the table, bringing him a mocha cappuccino. He simply stares at her and says nothing. Once she leaves, he grabs his pen and scribbles down a few more sentences and gives Princess of Havok a triumphant smile. "There. Done with that one."

"May I read some of your work sometime?" she asks, smiling back.

"Sure."

"Um, my friends are over there, by the counter. Would you like to meet them?"

And it's that easy. Mortys continues to come down to the coffeehouse every day, and he often hangs out with the friends. Sometimes, though, he tells them he'd feel more comfortable alone, and he goes back to his corner. It's happened twice a week so far, leaving a mysterious air about him.

One night, when school's finally out, the friends decide to do something that will test their friendship and trust. It will also test their honesty. Unan doesn't protest because she has no idea what questions Alexey has cooked up to ask everyone. They invite Mortys along; he says it will probably help them get to know him better.

That night, around eleven, they meet at the coffeehouse. There is a microphone on the stage and a small stool made of wood. A homemade sign stands on the side, proudly displaying the names of those who are to be present tonight. At the bottom, there is a large WELCOME, and underneath,

42

Mortys, in incredibly creepy writing. When Princess of Havok arrives with Alexey – who's better now and helped decorate the coffeehouse – Unan greets them at the door.

"I can't believe the work you guys put into this!" she cries. "I was so surprised when I came in." Alexey shrugs, and Havok grins from ear to ear.

"You proud? I bet nobody can wait to hear sexy Alexey's questions," she says, slyly.

"Did you look already?!! That's not fair!"

"No, I didn't. But they've gotta be good. He wouldn't do anything with me all day because he was writing them," Princess of Havok explains. He lays a hand on her already messed-up hair and rubs it back and forth.

"Sorry, Havok. Didn't mean to blow you off," he apologizes, kindly. He has always been so gentle and good-natured with her. "Where's Dave?"

"Oh, he's on his way. I hope Mortys shows up. This could be really nifty," Unan says, wiping off the counter. The late help left early, so she had to close the coffeehouse down at ten thirty and clean everything herself.

About five minutes later, everyone is assembled in front of the stage. Mortys is sitting on the floor in Dave's favorite cross-legged style.

"Okay, everybody, I think we're ready to begin," Alexey announces through the microphone. "I will read the questions, and then you will all answer, one by one. I'll answer when all of you are finished. The rules are: you have to respond as truthfully as possible. If there's anything you really don't want us to know, you don't have to say it, although that takes away from the fun and trust in the exercise. So, let's begin."

"May we all learn not only about others, but maybe even more about ourselves," Mortys calls out.

FIRST QUESTION: WHAT DO YOU DO FOR FUN?

Nobody stands up to go first. Everyone looks around at each other, expecting someone else to go. Finally, Dave stands up and heads toward the microphone.

"For fun, I like to just hang out with the people that I'm close to. But in the privacy of my own home, I listen to music. And..." He stops to sit on the stool and starts motioning with his hands. "As I lay on my bed, I listen carefully to the words and let them flow straight through my body. It's like I can better interpret the meanings of the songs," he explains, excitedly, staring off into space. He blinks, realizing he's finished, and steps down almost embarrassedly. Princess of Havok gets up, hesitantly, and sits on the stool. She doesn't begin speaking until she's comfortable.

"Hi, my name is Princess of Havok," she introduces herself, laughing. She gets a response from the audience and then goes on. "I usually spend my time with Unan. We talk and sometimes go to my friend Kermie's soccer games. Sometimes I spend time with my other friend, Boo, but that's a different story. Um... I like to piss the preps off. I'll wear ugly, mismatching clothes or let my music play loudly in public. And there's one more thing I do. I like to mess with guys' minds. I know that probably makes me sound like some kind of slut or something, but please hear me out. I... God, I don't even know how to explain it. I usually do it to guys that know they can never have me because I dislike them. Other times, I do it to get to know a guy and make sure he has more personality than a rock. Take Alexey and Dave for example. I mean, neither of them came across as pigs or anything. They played along for a bit, sure! But then they actually showed interest in getting to know *me*. That's what I'm looking for. And if I ever do anything like that now to Alexey, Dave, or even you, Mortys, you gotta know that I'm just doing it in good fun. I hope you don't mind my joking around like that. Oh... I guess there's another time when I do this. Uh..." She starts to blush, looking down, ashamed. "Well, when I'm depressed or something, I sorta do it then, too. I guess..." She sighs. "I guess it just makes me feel better to know I have the power. I don't know." She gets off the stool and walks over to Alexey, apologetically. He puts a finger to the end of her lips, and she smiles, holding onto his hand. She sits back down. Mortys stands up next. Once he gets there, he seems accustomed to being on the stage.

"Well, first of all, I'd like to say that it was pretty cool the way Havok was able to confess all of that. I can tell by the way you say everything that you all trust each other to the extent that you know nobody in this room will condemn you for what you're saying," he says. "Okay. Anyway... You all know what I like to do. I come here and sit in a corner, by myself, and write. That is, when I'm not talking to all of you. But I've had a lot of people ask me what I'm writing, and I don't often tell them because most wouldn't understand. I watch the people walking in and out of the coffeehouse. And sometimes, I'll see human beings that just disgust me by being in the room. A girl whose hair is too blond. A guy who smiles constantly. I think you know what I mean. So, I sit there and let my hatred stew. Then, I create the worst death imaginable, in my head, for them to live out. So that's what I write. I explain their death, to the fullest detail, and make sure everything gory gets thrown in. Where we used to live, there weren't many people to see, so I just wrote stories about anything controversial. Come to think of it, I didn't get out a whole lot back home. But now, I have all these wonderful people to kill. In my stories, I mean," he finishes. He steps down and resumes his position on the floor. Unan gets up, timidly, and stands near the microphone. She holds a banana, tightly.

"Hehe. Hi," she says quietly. She's not afraid of her friends, but the thought of being up on a stage has never really thrilled her, either. Everyone's smiling at her shyness. She runs a hand over her flattening spikes. "I basically just spend time with Havok. And everybody else here," she quickly adds, trying not to exclude anyone. "I can't really say I do anything intelligent like try to figure out the meaning of life. I... I think I spend more time confused than anything else," she explains, frowning. "Um, that's all." Unan sits back down, looking disappointed at having just discovered this. A new revelation for her.

"I hang out with all of you lovely people. Other than that, I like to write. Poetry, mainly. And I like creating programs for my computer. But you guys all forgot one important thing we love to do!" Alexey cries. They all give each other questioning looks.

"Oh! Our mini-RPGs!" Princess of Havok yells out. "At the good old cabin! I can't believe we forgot!"

SECOND QUESTION: WHAT DO YOU HATE MOST ABOUT PARENTS?

"I'll go first!" Mortys cries. "Their existence. And the fact that they brought me into this world."

"I'd have to agree," Dave replies. "I would have said the same thing." Unan stands up and takes the mike.

"Now that I'm used to this stage thing... mine were never there for me. Not in the way I would have liked them to be. Sure, they were always there to tell me what to do and shit like that. Well, what about when I learn to think for myself? When I know how to decide what to wear and what to do with my time. They're still trying to force ideas into my head. I hate that! Of course, I suppose that's why I'm living here instead of with them, right? Anyway, that's what I hate the most. They try to live your life for you." They all clap, and Unan bows with a large smile on her face. Princess of Havok is next, and she takes her time walking onto the stage.

"Parents suck in the most inexplicable ways. But I'd have to say that I hate them the most when they tell me they understand what I'm going through. Which is a bunch of bullshit because then they can't even listen to you when you try to tell them what kind of crap you had to go through at school today. You know, about the kid who spit at you, the girls who taunted you, or even the guy that wanted to rape you. They say they care, when I think they couldn't care less! Why the hell do you want to tell your kids to talk to you about their lives when you're not even gonna listen?!!" she cries. She stops; she hadn't meant to get so angry in front of everyone. "Anyway, that's only one of the reasons why I hate my parents." Princess of Havok steps down and allows Alexey to speak.

"I agree with everything you said. Looks like we have something in common. Okay, on to the next question!" he says, excitedly.

THIRD QUESTION: ARE YOU A VIRGIN?

"Feel free to go into as much detail as you feel is necessary," Alexey announces, smiling mischievously. They all laugh. Since nobody goes up, Mortys volunteers.

46

"No, I am not a virgin. Um... yeah. I think that's all you need to know," he explains. They boo, jokingly, and he simply shrugs. Dave decides to go next.

"Okay, I know you guys won't make fun of me, so yeah. I am. I had the opportunity, but I turned it down and don't even regret it to this day. The girl... man, she was gorgeous. And ready and willing. But then I figured, why? Just because she was good-looking? Just to say I'd done it? It wasn't worth it because she was a bitch to me anyway. She never talked to me again after that," Dave explains, calmly. They can tell from his expressions that he's not the least bit sorry about it. Princess of Havok dares to continue the discussion.

"Yeah. I'm a virgin. Sure, I've been hit on. A few guys wanted me, but they were the bastards that I hated. I dunno. Maybe I'm just a fuck-up looking for comfort about whether or not people want me that way," she laughs, though she's not quite sure if she's serious or not. Unan is last before Alexey, and she's debating how she should tell everyone. But why not just tell them the truth? That was what this was all about. She makes her way up to the stool and sits down, quietly. Unan takes a deep breath and begins.

"Just a couple weeks ago, I lost my virginity to a guy I met that same day. I don't think it was willingly, but don't get me wrong. It wasn't rape. He had seemed so perfect. I wasn't thinking straight. Not only that, but I hadn't eaten all day, and I took two Extra Strength Tylenol and one Advil. That's why I say it wasn't willingly. So one thing led to another," she sighs. "And I woke up with a sheet around me and a damn stranger in my bathroom. I could go on regretting it until the day I die, but that wouldn't solve anything. I guess I just learned my lesson." She hurries down to the floor. She sits on the ground, cross-legged, with her thumb in her mouth and rocks back and forth like an autistic child. Dave comes over and sits behind her, hugging her like the world's about to end. They take a short break from the questions, and everyone sips on some wine. It helps to calm Unan's nerves, and eventually, they are ready to go on. It's Alexey's turn.

"Okay, well... I'm not. Which pisses me off because I may as well have waited. It was this girl... obviously," he laughed. "She had this beautiful, long, black hair. God, I can't even begin to describe her. It was like we had so much in common. So, eventually, we... well, you know. About a week later, I saw her and she'd completely changed. She cared too much about her hair and her skin and the way she walked. She turned into every other girl at our school. And then she started hanging around this other guy. Damn basketball player. Anyway, I thought she cared so much. But the witch didn't even have the decency to say 'we're through.' Never dumped me. Just started seeing that other guy. I'm okay now. I still can't believe someone could be so insensitive, but I've found someone now that's twice as caring as that other girl could ever be. I can move on because this new person is beautiful inside and out, and *that* makes all the difference." He finishes, walking away from the microphone. He smiles at Princess of Havok, whose eyes look a tad watery.

FOURTH QUESTION: WORST/WEIRDEST/SCARIEST EXPERIENCE

"I think I'll go first," Princess of Havok says from the couch. She goes up onto the stage and sits down. "You know my friend Boo, who I said was a whole other story? Well, this has to do with her. I met her when her dad had just died. Anyway, she'd been getting into heroin, and I tried my best to keep her away from it. Not that easy. So I figured, alright, I'm sure she'll quit eventually because she's not stupid enough to get hooked. One day, I went over to her house to pick her up for Kermie's birthday party. Her mom was out with a guy, as usual, so I let myself in and walked into the basement, where Boo lives. I didn't see her at first, but the TV was on. I thought maybe Laxy-Boy, her boyfriend, was over, but it was really quiet. I went into her bedroom, and there she was, lying on the floor." Princess of Havok pauses to wipe away a tiny pool of tears in the corner of her eye. She takes a deep breath to try and calm her shaking voice. "I didn't know what to do. She looked so peaceful there, even though her veins were so deep blue, pulsating underneath her tissue-thin skin. You would've thought she was sleeping, but I saw the needle lying next to her. I called 911 and then Laxy-Boy, because I thought he had a right to know about it. While I waited, I didn't know what to do with myself " She sniffles and wipes her eyes again. "So I went back into her bedroom and sat down on the floor. I kissed her eyelids, pulled her head onto my lap, and rocked her back and forth, telling her everything would be alright. But I didn't know. She could have died or suffered brain damage. But she lived, and she was lucky. Nothing wrong. She's right back to it, though, and maybe that's why I'm not as close to her as I used to be. I'd have to say that was one of the scariest moments in my life." She steps down, solemnly, and goes to the back room to get a tissue. When she comes back, Unan prepares herself to go.

"I already told you about my experience a couple weeks ago. Well, that's my worst so far. It wasn't because I wasn't ready, though. It's because of who it was. Some guy I'd just met! And then I thought... I thought I could *trust* him. And now I just feel like I can never trust anyone again. Like I should stay away from relationships that could lead to sex or even any relationship at all with a guy. I don't know if I can completely trust people ever again." Dave gets up and heads for the bathroom. "So that was my worst experience so far. I don't think I need to explain any further." Unan sits back down, and Mortys takes the stage.

"I can clearly remember the weirdest thing that ever happened to me, but I'm not sure if I can describe it enough for anyone to understand. It was about a year or two ago. I was forced into going camping with my family in our shitty trailer. I had planned on spending the summer down in the subway station in the next city, writing or terrorizing people. Anyway, once we were camping, it wasn't too bad. But one day, we went into town for lunch, and I saw all these damn sheep. These people were all so alike and so happy it was utterly disgusting. I attempted to hit on this one girl who was a bit different from the rest, but she totally blew me off. She was so rude; she might as well have taken my body and snapped it in two. By the time we got back to the campground, I was so angry at this whole lie of a life. I could feel it burning inside me. All these stupid people, and I was stuck in the middle of it. I felt like I was gonna explode if I didn't get away. So I went to this one spot out on the water where I'd occasionally watch the sunset. It was a stone breakwater, but it went out pretty deep, and the sun had already gone down. And I remember looking out onto the water, feeling so frustrated with the world and people. They were always so happy, but there was no reason to be! I wondered why I wasn't stupid like them. Why couldn't I just live my life without worrying about money or how corrupt the fucking government is or anything like that." He is staring off into space again, clenching his fists. "It was pretty silent except for the waves breaking against the stone; they looked very inviting. It was almost as if the lake was calling out to me, the way the wind was whipping my clothes around. And I thought for a brief moment: why the hell am I here? Was there some purpose in me finding this spot? And the lake looked so infinite because you couldn't see the land on the other side. Maybe if I jumped in and didn't swim, everything would be okay. The waves would embrace me and keep me safe from the world. All these thoughts just started flying through my head, coming out of nowhere. But I snapped out of it when I started to wonder how long it would take my dead body to drift the length of the lake for someone to find it. That's my weirdest experience." He steps down, completely unfazed by what he's just shared with them. Everyone is still trying to absorb what he said. Dave is still in the bathroom, and nobody can figure out what's wrong with him. Alexey walks over there and tries to get him out while everyone takes a break.

Eventually, Dave comes out of the bathroom but still won't let anyone know what's wrong. He goes up on the stage.

"Scariest thing that's happened to me... I guess, well, things aren't supposed to scare guys, right?" he laughs. "And they're not supposed to cry, either. I've been scared, and I've cried, so I guess I broke the rules. I'm gonna say that it was the riot. The one over the sports complex. It wasn't the fact that we were there, and also not because we were standing up for what we believed in. It was when everything started getting violent. There was the four of us: Alexey, Havok, Unan, and me. And the people in the crowd, so many of them! It was like a mosh pit gone wrong, and I couldn't see

Unan. I couldn't believe these people hated us so much that they probably would have killed us had they gotten the chance. People coming at me with rocks and glass... I had to watch my friends go down, so I figured maybe I could still save Unan. I was afraid she was going to get hurt. I was afraid *everyone* would get hurt, but... well, I know that Unan sometimes gets a little confused. No offense or anything. I mean, she said it herself, and I knew that. I thought maybe she'd forgotten where she was or something. That's why I was frightened. I hope that doesn't sound mean." He steps down, almost seeming angry with himself. Unan can't believe that he actually understands her. She motions for him to come over to the couch, and she sits next to him, hanging onto his arm.

"Thanks for understanding me. I... I guess I should know of all people, I can trust my friends. And now, *especially* you," Unan whispers. It is all that needs to be said; Dave is no longer angry, and he's alright for the rest of the night. Alexey walks over to the microphone.

"I'd have to say the riot, too. I've had confrontations before, but not quite like that. Not with the majority of the school on the other side. All those people coming at me. Some had bottles, broken glass, rocks or stones, and some with just their bare hands. I mean, I was ready to be crucified after seeing some of the looks on their faces, like Dave was saying. But I made it through alright. Having friends there helped, and they especially made a difference by coming to visit me in the hospital." He takes a break, then goes on. "Okay, folks. Last question!"

FIFTH QUESTION: BEST/HAPPIEST EXPERIENCE

Mortys takes the stage, but doesn't bother to sit down.

"This one won't take too long. Even though I'm not a happy person. Like I was saying earlier, I never really had any friends or even got out that much back home. I like this place a lot more, most obviously the fact that I have my own apartment now. It's also a new place for me to call home. Yeah, before I was with my family, but what kind of home is that? Here I have friends and feel welcome. That sounds more appealing to me. So, my best experience would be meeting all of you. You could say we barely know each other because we met not too long ago. But I would have to argue with that statement. After tonight, I feel like I've known you all my life. Without you guys, I probably never would have known the meaning of true friends." He gets a round of applause and sits down on the floor. He goes into a classic pose, stretching out and crossing his long legs, leaning back and holding himself up with his arms. Unan stands up and takes over the microphone.

"Hi. It's me again." She's excited, still in awe that Dave understands her. He looks really attractive, even from up on stage. Like a guardian angel. She giggles at the thought and bites down on her lip, gently. "This'll sound mean at first, but listen to everything I have to say. The best experience of my life was meeting Havok. But I'm not excluding anyone!" she adds, quickly. "Because if I hadn't met her, I wouldn't have met everybody else here, either. And that would've sucked major hookie." Put in a way only Unan could put it. She gives everyone a smile bright as sunshine and goes back to the couch. Princess of Havok sits where she is.

"Ditto. My best experience is meeting all of you... and my other friends. But mostly all of you because you're who I spend most of my time with, and you're always there for me. I love you guys." Nobody else gets up. Alexey and Dave simply nod and agree.

"I'd have to say this was all very productive. Well, thank you for coming! Maybe we can do this again," Alexey suggests.

As they file out the door – all except Unan – they decide that it's about time to do another mini-RPG. Mortys says he would love to tag along, if that's okay with them. But when they call him to let him know when they're going, he's changed his mind. Apparently, he had been playing his music a little too loudly. The woman downstairs warned him about it and eventually called the police. When the police went to his apartment, and he opened the door, they said he "looked suspicious" and demanded to come in. He let them in without a fuss. When they made their way inside, they found that he had been making absinthe in the comfort of his own home, which is illegal. However, they couldn't do anything about it because they didn't have the right to search his apartment in the first place. But he felt it would be better to maybe leave the city for a little bit. Perhaps even the state. Not so much because of the incident with the police, but more so because he needed more material for his writing.

So, as Mortys was leaving the state to discover new places and expand his writing, the original four were on their way to a cabin just outside of town.

"Really Pathetic Game" and a Girl in the Woods

It is stuffy in Dave's car. It's an old Honda, and they all have just enough room inside. The rain is hitting the roof, and it almost puts Unan to sleep.

"Can you turn up the air?" she asks, quietly.

"Sorry, love, it's up as high as it'll go," Dave replies, turning off the freeway and onto the exit ramp. He seems distant, but probably only because he's driving. The Specials are playing quietly in the background. Unan turns to see how Princess of Havok is doing; she's sleeping, snoring quietly. Her head is resting lightly between the edge of the seat and the window. She clutches her sweater vest in her hands.

"How's Havok doing back there?" Alexey asks.

"She's sleeping." When they hit a bump, she wakes up with a start, sitting up straight. She looks out all the windows, realizes they're still not there, and falls back against the seat. Unan almost laughs as Princess of Havok stretches, clawing helplessly at the air.

"Are you up now?" she giggles.

"Yeah, I think so." She thinks for a moment. "It's hot in here."

"I know. I'm doing the best I can," Dave announces.

"It's okay." Alexey turns around and looks at Havok. She stares back, silent.

"Are you alright?" he questions. She makes a face.

"I feel sick."

"Don't worry. We're almost there," he replies.

"Yeah, I know." They turn down the dirt road that leads to the cabin. Alexey turns back to the front. Havok slumps over next to Unan. Seeing the look on Havok's face, she holds onto her head and pulls it to her, messing up her hair. "I feel like shit," she mumbles, allowing Unan to hold her. "If I puke on you, don't hold it against me."

"I won't," she replies, laughing. As they near the cabin, the rain gets even harder. It'll probably be a pain in the ass to get their stuff inside. When they finally get there, it's downright pouring. Dave stops the car and nobody moves.

"Well..."

"Havok, get inside. I don't want you to get any sicker than you already are," Alexey announces. "Hey, Dave, got any umbrellas?"

"No, sorry."

"Here, take this," Unan says, giving them her MTX work shirt. Princess of Havok manages a small smile, and Alexey helps her out of the car and into the cabin.

Once everything is inside, they decide to start a fire. Although it's summer, the temperature outside is much lower than out beyond the woods, and the rain has made it even cooler. The cabin is freezing because it is so deep into the woods that it never gets any sun. Anyway, as soon as the fire's started, Princess of Havok takes a blanket and lies right next to it.

"I hope she's not gonna be sick tomorrow."

"We could just start a little later than we expected."

"Shit. I don't want her sleeping on the floor like that." That was Alexey. He goes into the bedroom and pulls out one of the cots. As he's trying to open it, Unan and Dave simply look on. He wakes her up and gets her to move from the floor to the makeshift bed. Once she's on it, though, he doesn't bother to come back and talk to Unan and Dave. He instead sits in front of the fire, on the floor next to her, and strokes her hand gently.

The night goes by uneventful. When Unan wakes up from the chair she was sleeping in, she looks around to see if anyone else is awake yet. Dave is still asleep on the couch in the cabin, and Alexey has a cot pushed up next to Havok's. However, Havok is not there. Unan is about to panic, but then she hears crackling in the kitchen. She stands up, nearly tripping over her own pajama pants, and walks over. There, she finds Princess of Havok standing at the stove, already dressed.

"Good morning, almighty Unan!" she cries. Unan gives her a questioning look. "Breakfast," she replies, cheerfully giggling. "Bacon and eggs. I went to the store this morning."

"Without a license?"

"Hells yeah!" They both laugh.

"Nobody's up yet."

"Ah well. We'll just have to wake them up when it's ready."

"I take it you're feeling better."

"*Much* better. Definitely." She pokes at the eggs with a spatula. "I hope I did this right."

"That's comforting!" a drowsy Dave calls out. He stumbles over to the kitchen, rubbing his eyes. Unan can't believe how wonderful he looks in his flannel pajama bottoms and a long-sleeve, black shirt. "Hey, Alex still isn't awake."

"I'll tend to that. Could you guys please put the eggs and bacon on the paper plates?" They nod. "Cool." She wipes her hands on a paper towel and bounces over to Alexey's cot. She seems to full of life and energy today. She sits next to him and runs a hand through his hair. "Hey, sexy. Wake up." He stretches, groggily, and opens his eyes to look up at Princess of

Havok.

"You're all better?"

"Yeah," she laughs. "C'mon, darling. I made breakfast."

"Uh-oh," he replies, joking around. He gets up, and they both make their way into the kitchen.

"Gross. We're going to sound like an old, married couple."

"Nah, we won't," he reassures her. But it seems as though there's something bothering him.

After breakfast, they decide to start the mini-RPG that Alexey has made for them. Unan the Conqueror – and warrior – must devise a strategy for war and take her army into the neighboring country. To represent the strategy, Alexey hands her a crossword puzzle. After she's finished with that, she will take her army – Dave – into the woods and kill a small bird with a slingshot.

"But if you feel uncomfortable with that, you could just take your sword up and scare some animals into running around," Alexey suggests. Her sword being a stick that she picked up off the ground. Meanwhile, Princess of Havok is being held captive, so Unan must do this without her sidekick. Then, they were all supposed to meet up in the tree house, a few hundred feet behind the cabin. "I'm sorry it's so fucking lame this time, but I haven't had much spare time to write it in. You guys were probably expecting something big and really creative," Alexey apologizes. They all tell him it's alright because it's something to do and start the game.

Unan sits outside with Dave pacing back and forth.

"What's a three-letter word for... oh, never mind." She scribbles something down quickly, sighs, taps the pencil against her leg, and turns the paper over. "Oh my God! There's another side! Do I have to do this one, too?" she asks, looking up at him. He stops walking.

"Knowing Alexey, you should probably do it just to be sure. Otherwise, he'll make up some excuse to take points away from you," Dave replies. "Do you want me to help you?"

"Please?" she pleads, looking at him, helplessly. "Besides, that way we'll get done quicker. Maybe I get extra points for that..." He sits down next to her on the ground.

While they work on the crossword puzzles and Unan's tasks, Alexey and Princess of Havok sit inside the cabin. It's quiet.

"So..."

"Are we just supposed to keep checking the tree house to see if they're done yet?" Princess of Havok asks.

"Yeah, I guess so." Silence. She pushes one of the cots up to the bedroom window and kneels on it, peeking out the window.

"Nope, not done yet," she giggles. It was a given, but there was nothing else to do anyway. She sits down, motioning for Alexey to come in the bedroom. He takes his place on the cot and leans up against the wall.

"So what do you want to do?"

"I dunno."

About five minutes later, they are fooling around on the cot, playfully pushing each other back and forth. They eventually start kissing, after Princess of Havok pretends to punch Alexey, and he grabs her hand, not letting go. She moves closer, trying to get her hand back. Alexey lets go, but at the same time leans into her, pressing his lips lightly against hers. She is caught by surprise at first, but quickly adapts to the situation. Alexey stops, smiling at her, and she grins back. They continue, and that's the funny part; they don't seem to stop. While they kiss, Havok slides her boots off and pulls her legs up onto the bed, crossing them. She wraps her arms around his neck, letting her hands snake up into his hair and pulling him even closer.

"Oh, wow," she murmurs, breathlessly. Alexey's lips drift toward her neck. "This is better than that stupid sex ed video they showed in anatomy." He laughs and lifts his head.

"They were so *old*..." he comments, kissing her again.

A few minutes later. They're still at it, only now they're lying down. Alexey has his shirt off, and it is almost more than Princess of Havok can handle. She stops to take off her sweater vest because it's becoming too hot in the cabin to need it. At least, in this room it is. Somehow, Alexey manages to reach her white shirt. He has the first three or four buttons undone. Havok stops for air, but she has no intention of finishing it here.

"Alexey?" she says, quietly.

"Mm-hmm?" he answers, having a feeling he knows what she's about to say.

"I---" She's stopped by a large banging noise outside. They both jump up from the cot and run outside. Dave and Unan are still by the side of the cabin, but they aren't sitting down anymore.

"What the hell was that?!" Alexey cries.

"It wasn't us," Unan replies, shrugging. "It came from over there." She points in the general direction left of them. They all walk, slowly, into the woods, but stop when they see a girl talking to what appears to be a can.

"Fuck you!" she screams at it, throwing it against a board. So that's where the banging came from. They all just stand there, unsure whether they should be frightened or amused. "Okay, let's try this again," she mumbles to herself, pulling a couple more pop cans out of a box. They can finally make out that they are cans of Mountain Dew. She holds them, one in each hand, out to each side. They are both still closed. Her back is to them, so they can't see much, but she seems to be in complete concentration. One of the cans begins to shake... and then it explodes open, Mountain Dew gushing out of the opening. "Yes!" she cries, lifting the cans higher into the air. The other can crumples in her hand. She throws both of them into the air. "Thank you!" she yells, throwing herself onto the ground, kissing a rock. She hugs it. "I love you, and I miss you dearly." By now, the friends are pretty surprised. So far, they've seen this girl talk to pop, make a can explode, and hug and kiss a rock. They don't know what to make of it.

"Holy shit," Dave says aloud. He quickly shuts his mouth, realizing just how loudly he said it. The girl gets up and turns around.

"Who are you?!" she screams. She has brown hair with white-blond strands next to her face. She is wearing a black shirt and postal pants. "Go away!" She gathers her things and looks at them once more. "And you! Put

60

some clothes on! It's not *that* warm out here," she adds, pointing at Alexey. She runs away.

"Hey, why *are* you guys so... undressed, anyway?" Unan asks. Dave clears his throat.

"I don't think you want to ask that," he replies.

"It's a long story," Princess of Havok says.

"I'll bet," Dave answers. Unan smiles, brightly.

"It's okay. We have plenty of time!" she cries.

"You know, maybe we should just take the rest of the day off. We can wait for another day to do this. Or wait until I can actually come up with a good idea. Besides, I have something to tell you guys. But I'll tell you later this evening. Why don't we just go drive around?" Alexey suggests. So they do.

While in town, they stop for gas and go to the store. There are a lot of people out in the warm weather, but the disgusting thing is they all seem to look the same. The friends split up; Alexey and Dave go to the store to buy food, and Unan and Princess of Havok slip into the park for a walk. They decide to hang out by a fountain, where a couple is seated on the gray rock.

"So?" Unan asks. She figures Princess of Havok will know what she's talking about.

"So what?" She picks a flower from the side of the fountain, snapping the head off and positioning it on her ear. "How do I look?"

"Wonderful," Unan replies. "Now, what were you and Alexey doing?" Princess of Havok seems to ponder about it for a moment.

"We just got a little carried away." A few people stop and stare at them. It's no different from being at home. She looks out onto the water.

"I see. Do you think you're gonna—" Unan is interrupted.

"I dunno. Maybe."

"I was just curious." Princess of Havok stands, stretching, and walks toward the water. Bodies are strewn all over the beach, lying out on towels and underneath umbrellas. A stereotypical sand scene.

"Did you ever notice how people say not to stereotype things because they're not all the same... but they are?" she asks Unan. She doesn't respond, simply following Havok. They walk out onto a pier. Dave and Alexey are following them, having just gotten done shopping. Havok sits at the end, taking off her boots and striped socks, and lets her legs dangle into the clear water. Unan leans against a wooden railing while Alexey and Dave approach them.

"Everything's in the car already."

"What are you doing?" Alexey asks. Havok doesn't even bother to turn and speak to him, mesmerized by the sparkling waves.

"Enjoying the fresh air?" Unan answers, unsure of the truth.

"May I join you?" Havok pats the spot next to her, and he sits down. She moves closer and leans against him, but a breeze floats past and pushes the flower from her ear.

"Oh no!" she cries, leaning forward to pry it from the grasp of the water. Instead, she tumbles in, making a huge splash.

"Havok!" Alexey yells, jumping up onto his feet and backing away from the edge. Unan laughs, giddily, and jumps in after her. Princess of Havok surfaces, running a hand over her face to clear away water.

"Haha! Aw, man. Christ, that was funny!" she cries. She can't stop laughing. Unan pops up next to her.

"Hi! It looked like fun, so I thought I'd join you."

"You guys are insane! Do you realize you're fully clothed? You're crazy!"

"Thank you!" Havok replies. "Now I know my sexy Alexey wants to take a dip..." she says, pulling on his leg. He sits down again.

"Fine. But I'll at least have the decency to take off my shirt first," he replies. He then lets her pull him in. Dave crosses his arms over his chest.

"Oh, alright. I guess I'm the last one left!" He dives in. They now have an audience, for some reason disgusted at their actions. Then again, they're not your stereotypical beach-goers. They don't show their appreciation quietly; they are also having fun, even if looking immature by doing so. Who cares what everyone else thinks? They don't feel the need to show

62

everyone how "good" they are, or how cool, or how tan. They don't care.

As they walk back to the car, in sopping wet clothes, Alexey springs the news on them.

"I think we should do this every year," Dave announces. Alexey stops walking and sighs.

"I was gonna wait to tell you guys about this, but I can't any longer. You need to know. I'm going back to Russia when we get back. We may even have to leave earlier than I expected," he says. He continues moving and refuses to look at anyone. Princess of Havok doesn't say another word all the way back to the cabin.

That evening, they have a visitor. The strange girl from the woods shows up with an offering: a TV. She marches right through the front door with it.

"I'm sorry I scared you people earlier. I didn't mean to. I just haven't seen much civilization lately. I've been living out here for a while, kinda isolating myself, I guess. Anyway, could I put this down somewhere?" she asks, impatiently. They set it down on a table. She seems to be sharing a lot, but it's to be expected if she's been out here by herself for so long. "I'm... well, if you had to label me, I guess you'd call me a witch. Um, people used to call me Goddess of Carbonation, my specialty, but it never really stuck too well, and my actual name is Midnight. Could I sit down and watch TV with you?" She is edgy, a little jumpy for this time of the day. "I came out here when my love was killed. His friend killed him... some RPG business... but the kid was too wrapped up in his character. He... well, he hung him. You don't know pain until you see that. Someone's neck snapped and their face purple and... do you have anything to drink?"

"In the refrigerator," Dave replies, intrigued by the newcomer. She looks through, but doesn't find anything to her liking, shaking her head.

"No, I meant a *drink*. None of this soft shit."

"There's brandy in the cupboard above the stove." She pulls it out and brings the whole bottle with her to the chair she is sitting in.

"So I moved away from everything. Because I know he's here with me. He is! I can feel him in nature, in my mind, in every step I take while hiking

63

through the woods. My poor Dorian." She takes a swig of the brandy. Princess of Havok glares at Alexey and walks outside. She finds a clearing where she can lay down the look up at the stars. There are plenty of them, so beautiful and bright. How deceiving. Nothing on earth was like that. No more. No more will she listen to anyone she thinks she trusts. Nothing is what it seems... what it appears to be. Nothing...

"You're angry with me," Alexey says, coming up behind her.

"I have every right to be." She follows the light of an airplane in the sky with her eyes. They're burning with frustration, and light smoke appears as she speaks. He doesn't respond. The noise from the TV in the cabin reaches their spot.

"Have I ever told you you're as gorgeous as those stars in the sky? As wonderful as the full moon on a clear night?" Alexey asks, quietly. She begins to cry.

"Is that why you're leaving?"

"No. I—"

"Don't tell me now! It won't do any good anymore! You're fucking *leaving me* here! How do you expect me to feel?! How can you possibly wonder why I'm angry?" she asks, standing up to face him.

"Okay. Maybe you don't believe me, but I love you," he replies, whispering. He reaches toward her head, attempting to brush away twigs. "Havok?" She runs away from him, heading back to the cabin.

"Don't touch me again!"

Princess of Havok enters the cabin, and nobody says anything. Dave and Unan pretend they don't notice – because they don't want to interfere – and keep their eyes glued on the TV. She sits on the couch, where no one else is seated. Alexey walks in a few minutes later, running a hand through his hair and acting as though he wouldn't hesitate to pull it out any second. He sighs and treads around in a circle, his face distorting, looking like he's about to smash something. Instead, he begins to cry. He's not sobbing, but tears roll down his face. He dematerializes before their eyes and falls onto the couch and onto Havok's shoulder. She is surprised at the intrusion, but it hurts her to see him so weak. He's never been like this before, except on his first day at the hospital. She can't help but put her arms around him, but he makes barely any response. She is suddenly bombarded by an army of "I'm sorry"s erupting from Alexey's mouth and onto her clothing.

"Stop," she pleads. "Stop that!" He falls onto her lap, clutching at his face. She moves a bit so that he can lie down. "*I'm* sorry. I shouldn't be upset. I never even allowed you a chance to explain." Princess of Havok pets his hair and runs a hand over his cheek. "But you're still leaving me," she adds, trying not to get caught up in the moment and cry again.

"Perhaps I should leave now," Midnight, the strange visitor comments. She stands and fixes her pants. "You guys can hang onto the TV until you leave. It was nice talking to you." She leaves as quickly as she burst in.

"Dammit, she took the brandy bottle with her," Dave replies to the shutting of the door. Despite the tension in the cabin, they all laugh. Alexey finally stands up and wipes his face with a long hand.

"I think I'm gonna go to bed. Is it alright if I take the bedroom?" Nobody disagrees with him, and he heads in there and shuts the door behind him. Princess of Havok continues to sit on the couch, not speaking. She stares at the floorboards while the television blares something unintelligible. Maybe TV's actually utter gibberish when nobody's listening...

"I'm gonna share the bedroom with Alexey... I don't want him to be alone. Now that he thinks I hate him," she explains. Unan nods, a sympathetic string tugging at her heart.

"You can take the cot if you want," Dave adds, smiling.

"Okay. Thanks." She pushes the extra cot into the room, and Alexey gladly welcomes her. They keep the door shut.

"Well..." Dave sighs. "What an eventful day." He lies down on the wide couch and begins to flip channels. Unan uses the bathroom to change into boxers and a t-shirt from Salvation Army, even though it's cold. She reenters the living room, throwing her day clothes off to the side somewhere.

"Am I gonna sleep on the chair?" she asks, crossing her fingers for some sign that Dave just might be interested. He pretends to think about it for a moment.

"There's plenty of room on this couch... I guess." He smiles, and Unan melts into a little puddle of punk rock. "Besides, I bet it's a lot more comfortable." He opens up the blanket, ready for her to leap in next to him.

"Okay, okay. No need to persuade me." She climbs in, and Dave pulls the blanket over the both of them. They are both lying on their sides, Dave leaning against the couch back. "I take it there's nothing good on," Unan says. He laughs.

"Is there ever?"

"I don't watch much TV," she replies, stopping to ponder about it.

"Let's see... big corporations producing what the public wants with supposed actors and actresses who make millions of dollars for one single episode."

"I guess that's a no," Unan says, smiling. He messes up her hair.

"Silly girl." Dave laughs, flipping the channel once more. She attempts to readjust a little to get more comfortable, and her backside winds up sticking out a bit; it sinks into the indentation made by the ever-so-delicious area between Dave's stomach and knees. He doesn't say a word. The movie *IQ* is on, and the channel stays there. Dave throws down the remote. "It's set so that it'll go off in about an hour by itself. Is that alright?"

"Yeah." They lay in silence; no sound comes from the bedroom. Princess of Havok and Alexey must have been exhausted. Dave rubs his hand over Unan's arm lightly, a sign of friendly affection. She could almost fall asleep it feels so nice, but it is making her think of other things. While Meg Ryan and Tim Robbins kiss on the sailboat, Unan feels a hand gently squeeze her butt. She gasps and has to hold her breath to keep from making a noise. Dave laughs, quietly.

"I know all the dirty things you'd like to do," he whispers in her ear. It sounds strangely familiar. A book? Perhaps a poem... Alexey's writing? No, maybe a band, a song... Suddenly, she recognizes it.

"You're the fire in my thighs," she giggles, in a breathy voice. Dave kisses her ear and whispers into it yet again.

"Thanks a lot." He takes a deep breath and prepares to doze off.

"Oh, Da-ave," Unan calls.

"Yes?"

"Since when do you listen to Third Eye Blind?"

"Since when do *you*?" They both laugh, neither of them answering the question. "You must have heard it to know what it was from... even if you misquoted it." A few moments of silence pass by, and Dave can tell he has embarrassed Unan, even though he had not meant to. "Psst. Can I tell you a secret?" Dave asks.

"Sure. But it won't be a secret anymore," Unan giggles. She reaches down underneath the blanket and takes his hand in hers.

"I want you. Sshhhh..."

"I want you, too. I've wanted you ever since I saw your beautiful chest."

"Oh, I see. This is purely a physical attraction thing, right?" he asks. The TV still has not turned off yet. The starring couple is fighting.

"Of course!" Unan jokes. Dave kisses her cheek... then slowly continues down her neck to her collarbone and stops. She closes her eyes, gripping his hand, waiting for more. When nothing comes, she protests. "Don't—" she pleads.

"Stop?" Dave interrupts. "I have to, crazy Unan. If I don't, nobody will watch out for us. You're not ready for something like that. And... aw, hell, I care about you. Not tonight, conqueror. See you in the morning." Dave puts an arm around her waist and settles in for the night. She blinks a few times, looking around the dark room, trying to comprehend what he just said. He was right. She had told herself that she wouldn't do something like that so soon after what happened with Ryan. On TV, Meg Ryan and Tim Robbins are kissing in the open field where they'd gone to gaze at the stars. Unan smiles. Who ever said things like this only happened in the movies? She closes her eyes, and moments later, the television turns off.

The next morning, the friends pack up and prepare to leave because Alexey needs to leave the next day for Russia. After everything's in the car, they say goodbye to the good old cabin and take the TV back to Midnight.

Alexey carries the television set, and Dave knocks on the door.

"Yeah?" she opens the door and answers groggily. "Oh, it's you guys. Are you leaving already?!" Her eyes open wide. She opens the door to let them in, but nobody moves.

"We just came by to drop off the TV. We're leaving now," Dave explains.

"Just like that?!"

"Well... yeah..." Unan replies. They figure this girl really needs some company. Princess of Havok has an idea.

"Would you like to come with us?" she asks. Midnight goes into hysterics.

"No!!! No, no, no. *Completely* out of the question. No. Definitely not. No. Unh-unh. Nope. No, just... no, i-it's better this way. This... can I try something?" she says.

"Uh, okay," Alexey answers, shrugging. She holds her hands to her forehead and closes her eyes slowly. "Well, should I put the TV down?"

"No!" she cries. "Hold it, out in front of you if possible..." Everything gets quiet, and she concentrates. They all wait for some supernatural sign of incredible phenomena. It seems as though Alexey's struggling to hold the TV up, and then it breaks free of his grasp, floating. "I can handle it from here," she says, cringing. "No need to worry. I guess I'll see you guys again, someday. Take care!"

"Holy shit," Unan mutters. "A flying television set? I've gotta be seeing things!" She does the silly walk all the way to the car, mumbling "I'm insane" over and over again. Alexey laughs, and Havok hangs onto his arm.

"Yeah, something like that. We'll be back again sometime," she replies, giving Alexey a longing look. She still hasn't forgotten that he'll be leaving the very next day.

"You take care, too, alright?" Dave says. She nods and turns around slowly, shutting the door. They stand there for a few moments, reminiscing over happier times at the cabin. Suddenly, there is a loud crash from inside.

"Screw you, you stupid piece of big corporation, media shit!" Havok giggles, smiling at Alexey and Dave.

"I guess she dropped the TV." They hear her kicking things around.

"Dorian, where are you?!" she cries. They all look at each other.

"It's amazing how attached she is to him," Dave comments. An awkward silence passes by until Unan gallops by.

"Whee! Whee!" she laughs, giddily, enunciating the "h." Dave turns to her, incredulously. She giggles, childishly, trying to tickle him. He picks her up, swinging her around, and as her legs lift into the air, she screams.

"Watch out, you might break her," Havok jokes. Dave eventually puts Unan down, and she begins interpretive dancing.

"What the hell did you get into this morning?!" he cries.

"Nothing! I'm high on Dave!" she squeals, smiling from ear to ear. She does a high jump and kicks her leg into the air.

"Punk rock, baby! Punk fuckin' rock!" Princess of Havok yells, doing the same. She lets go of Alexey and follows Unan, running to the car.

When they return, Dave drops off Havok and Alexey at his house. On the way to the coffeehouse, Dave stops at Meijer to resupply Unan with bananas. When they finally get home, she asks him to stay.

"Well... I don't know. Don't you want to rest, or... be alone or something...? I..." It's not like Dave to stutter or stammer. There must be something wrong.

"No, I don't. C'mon, Dave! Bring in some CDs or something. That way, we'll have something to do," Unan replies. "Please?" He sits in the car and thinks about it while she has half her body leaning inside the car.

"I..." He sighs. Nothing else escapes from his lips.

"What can I do to at least make you stay a while? We can listen to whatever you want. We have tons of caffeine... and maybe some alcohol stashed away somewhere," Unan tries to tempt him. He doesn't move or make a noise. Then, he turns the car off and grabs a CD case.

"Okay."

"Yay!" she cries, jumping around. "I mean... alright, that's cool." He laughs and walks inside with her.

Midnight finds them up and talking; the lights are off, and an eerie glow floats around the stage from lit candles on the floor. Tool plays in background.

"I can't believe Alexey's leaving," Dave comments. "He didn't even tell *me*. I don't know why he waited so long to say something." Unan pokes at the wooden floor of the stage with her finger.

"Maybe he didn't want us to have so long to worry about it." Dave gives her a confused look. "I mean, the sooner he would have told us, the longer we would have had to think about it, and how much it's gonna suck, and how it's going to affect us. Do you get what I'm trying to say?"

"Yeah, I think so. This way, it's over and done with before we have a chance to say or do anything about it, right?"

"Right." She pauses for a moment. "I'm gonna miss him."

"I know what you mean. God, he was like my *only* friend for a while. But I still have you and Havok. And Mortys, if he ever comes back. I think... no, nevermind," Dave says, shaking his head.

"No, what?"

"Nothing, forget it." She tries to study his face, but instead of looking at her, he stares up at the ceiling. "It's embarrassing."

"Dave! How is it possible that there's still stuff you can't talk to me about? Me, of all people. Just tell me. I won't laugh. I accept you for who you are." He smiles at her.

"You're right. I was just gonna say that maybe... maybe I have a fear of being alone. But I don't have to worry about that, do I? My conqueror will take care of me," he laughs. She giggles.

"Of course I will!" She gets up and throws her fist into the air. "I will use my army if I must! No one shall harm Dave in any way. No forces of darkness, nor any crappy people at school. I will prevail!"

"Silly girl."

"Is that what you're going to call me from now on?" she asks.

"Yeah. Silly girl." Unan thinks for a moment, then starts toward him, doing the silly walk again.

"Silly Girl to the rescue!" she cries, giggling. She falls to the floor next to him, looking up. "Haha, I can see your nose hairs." He squeezes his nose shut with his hand.

"Hey, stop that," he says, in a nasally voice. He runs a hand along her cheek, and she blushes.

"I wonder what Alexey and Havok are doing."

The next morning, Unan wakes up before Dave. She dresses, quickly, and goes to pick up Princess of Havok, walking down the same sidewalk she always has. From outside, you wouldn't be able to tell something was wrong. It wasn't like the world had changed. It still looked the same, she still acted the same... weird, how life was.

"What am I talking about? Life? Shit, I'm becoming an intellectual or something," she mutters to herself. As she picks her wedge, two preps turn the corner. They are wearing flares and tank tops.

"Eww, it's that freak from school," one says to the other. Unan hears them and begins jumping up and down, waving both hands in the air.

"Yeah, I'm from your school! Hey, bitch!!! Wassup?!!" she screams across the street.

"Would you, like, go away, you... um... weirdo?" Unan stops and hangs her head, shaking it back and forth.

"No, no, no. I'm afraid I can't do that," she replies. She looks up, suddenly, giving them the evil eye. She starts across the street, walking slowly.

"Ohmygod! Like, go *away!*" one prep yells. They both run away, screaming, and Unan stops, laughing so hard she almost cries.

"Hahaha! *Fuck you!* I'm the conqueror. My army shall prevail!" she cries, triumphantly. She readjusts her spiked bracelet and continues her walk to Alexey's house to pick up Princess of Havok.

When Unan arrives, it looks as though nobody's awake. She hopes she didn't come too early, but she misses her sidekick and is eager to see her. Maybe both her and Alexey are feeling better now. She hops up the steps and knocks on the door.

"Hi!" Havok cries, coming to the door in a towel. "Come on in and sit down." She continues down the hallway while Unan lies on the couch, sprawling out. "I'll be right back. Just let me change." As soon as she disappears from sight, Alexey comes out in boxers, kicking something around, mumbling to himself.

"Shit, shit, stupid shit... oh, hey, Unan! How are you this morning?"

"Uh... good," she replies, checking out his chest. She giggles, quietly. His chest is *almost* as nice as Dave's. But Dave wants her. Unan smiles, shyly. "What's wrong?"

"Nothing, nothing at all." He attempts to turn the air conditioning up, and when nothing happens, he slams his fist against it. "Fuck you! Of all things, they turn off the goddamn air! Jesus Christ, I can't believe I'm moving back to Russia..." he mutters, looking down at the floor. He prepares to bang his head on the wall, but Unan leaps off the couch to stop him.

"Hey! Don't do that. Come sit down," she offers. He follows her back over to the couch and sits next to her.

"You think she hates me?"

"Of course not! She came to the door really happily this morning. You must have done *something* right," Unan replies. Alexey gives her a look... she has the feeling she knows what it means. "Oh... I see." He attempts to smile and laughs a little. "Still, she doesn't hate you. She loves you a lot. But we're all sad you're leaving."

"And I wish I could do something about that! Unan, you don't know how much I want to stay here. I don't want to go back to Russia. It wasn't *my* choice. If I could, I'd stay here with everything familiar to me... especially Havok. I can't believe this is happening. You don't understand how much I'm going to miss her. No, actually, I don't think *she* understands. I think maybe I've been taking her for granted. I never had a chance to show her just how much I love her. And now I'm leaving. I feel like if I really wanted to stay here, there must have been *some* way to make it happen," Alexey explains.

"Well, there's nothing you can do. And if she can't understand that, then

72

it's her own fault," Unan replies. "Are you ever going to come back and visit?" Alexey sighs and turns to gaze out the window.

"It doesn't look like that's going to be too great an option. And if I do, it would probably only be a couple times a year." Unan doesn't understand how they plan to stay together... "That's why it has to be over now. Between us. I couldn't expect her to stay faithful to me when I'm not only across the ocean, but I won't even be able to see her but twice a year or so. That wouldn't be fair to her. It's just gotta end." Princess of Havok comes out of the hallway, and they both stay quiet. Unan can't even look at her. Havok doesn't realize what they were talking about.

"Are you ready, Unan?"

"Yeah."

"You're leaving just like that?" Alexey asks. She shakes her head and goes to sit on his lap for the last time.

"Of course not."

"I'll go wait outside," Unan comments, flying out the door. Like a curious child, she peeks in the side window to catch a glimpse. She looks just as Alexey and Havok give each other a long kiss. She smiles. It's just as she thought. It seems as though all is right with the world again. Unan perches on the front step and waits for Princess of Havok. When she finally comes out, she's arguing with Alexey about whether or not she'll see him later at the airport.

"Don't do it, Havok. Don't you dare come to the airport later."

"If I didn't know any better, I'd think you didn't want to see me anymore," she jokes, skipping outside and turning around to face him. "I know we said goodbye, but I have to see you again before you leave."

"Dammit, I'm not kidding We already said goodbye without too much of a problem. If we have to do it again, you know it's just going to fuck things up," Alexey says. Havok simply laughs.

"Yeah, yeah, yeah. I'll see you later," she says, waving and starting to walk away. Unan follows her, hoping they don't start to fight again.

"Goddammit, you don't take me seriously! *Don't do it*!" Alexey yells down the street. He slams the door, and Unan cringes.

"C'mon, Unan," Princess of Havok calls. "Don't worry. He'll get over it." It looks as though nothing can dampen her good mood. Unan runs along beside her and begs Havok to tell her what happened last night.

Later that day, they are both hanging out around the coffeehouse. Dave left to take Alexey to the airport. Unan is hanging from the pole of an umbrella at one of the tables outside. Princess of Havok is throwing stones at passing cars' tires.

"Look at meeee!" Unan cries, swinging back and forth. "I'm *soooo* punk rock," she says, sarcastically. She starts to giggle when an old man in a car stops and rolls his windows down.

"Damn kids nowadays. Get off that umbrella! It's not your property!" he yells. By now, other cars are honking.

"Eeeeeeeat meeeeeee!" Unan says, smiling. "This *is* my property, dipshit." The man gives them a final, disgusted look and Havok flicks him off. He drives away. "Hey, when are we going to the airport?"

"Umm, now I guess. We might even be late! Oops..." Havok frowns. "Maybe he's right. Maybe I shouldn't go say goodbye again." They both think for a moment. "No, I have to. I love him too much." Unan grins. What a romantic story...

They take a cab to the airport. Running inside, tons of people stare at them. Unan's pants begin to fall down. She obviously forgot to put a belt on this morning.

"Wait, Havok!" she cries. She grabs her pants, wondering what they must look like: a girl in a blouse, skirt, and boots, and another running behind her in plaid pants that are falling down and a brown work shirt. What a sight. Unan wishes she could see it herself.

"We have to hurry up! What if he left already?" Havok cries, half turning to face Unan. Unan catches up, and they run into Dave.

"Hey, what are you two doing here?" he asks, grabbing Princess of Havok's arm and not letting her go any farther.

"Stop it, Dave! Let me go! I'm gonna miss him, I'm gonna *miss him!*" she yells, frantically. Unan scratches her head. For some reason, she's gone completely hysterical. Havok is never like this.

"No, I don't think so. He's not scheduled to leave for another half hour," Dave replies. He gives Unan a look, and she keeps her mouth shut. Princess of Havok relaxes a bit, and Dave lets go of her. She sighs, and when they're least expecting it, she continues running.

"Hahaha! You're lying!!!" she yells. More people stare. Dave sighs, Unan shrugs, and they both begin running after her. This time, Unan remembers to hold her pants up.

"She's gone completely mad," Dave comments.

"Is Alexey gonna be there when she gets to the gate?"

"You want the truth?" he replies, out of breath.

"Yeah."

"Probably not."

They eventually catch up to Princess of Havok. When they do, they find her standing at the large window.

"He's gone," Unan says.

"That's his plane leaving right now," Dave replies. Unan walks up behind her and holds her hand.

"It'll be okay," she whispers to Havok, who's shaking her head. Her clothes are messed up, and what hair she has is flying around her face.

"He told me. He told me not to come, and he was right about what he said would happen. It wasn't that he didn't want to see me," she explains. She squeezes Unan's hand, gently.

"What do you mean?" Unan asks. "I don't get it."

"He said I'd mess things up. And I did. For me."

"I'm really sorry, Havok," Dave apologizes. "You know I didn't want to stop you back there. I was just doing what Alexey asked me."

"I know. And I also know I can't dwell on this too long. It's over. It took me a while to realize that because I didn't want to acknowledge it. Figured if I didn't, it wouldn't be true. But I know now," Havok says, quietly.

"You're right. The best way is to just move on." Unan almost forgets where she is. Who knew this would happen? Who would have ever known Alexey would leave and things would change so much? This can't be happening... but it is.

"Yeah. But... just let me have at least one minute to grieve." She lets go of Unan, walking even closer to the glass. She places an outstretched hand on it and presses her face to the glass. As she slowly slides to the floor, a wet streak appears on the window. She sobs quietly, and the plane takes off for Russia.

The three friends that are left say nothing as their lives change. Yet another memory to add to their collection, never to be forgotten. The sun continues to shine, and the war goes on.

| Lintalicious

Since Havok's parents aren't expecting her home for another couple weeks – if at all – she decides to stay with Unan at the coffeehouse. They try not to say too much about their missing friend, and occasionally, Dave comes to visit.

"We need to go out and meet new people," Unan says one night.

"When have we *ever* gone out to meet new people?" Havok asks.

"I don't know, but it sounded like a good idea." Unan grabs some wine from behind the bar and hands it to Princess of Havok.

"Thanks. I guess maybe you're right. We need to make some more friends. Well, not necessarily *friends*. Wait... people don't get along well with us," Havok explains.

"No, I mean... we should meet new people somewhere we know they'll be cool." Suddenly, Dave storms in. He throws Princess of Havok a pyramid bracelet.

"Thank you! I don't have one of these yet," she replies, trying it on.

"No problem. Did you guys know there's a Rancid concert coming up soon? This weekend, actually," he announces. Princess of Havok jumps up.

"Are you shitting me?!!" she cries. Dave shakes his head and sits down next to Unan. "We need to get tickets!"

"No need at all. I already got 'em for you," he replies, smiling. As Unan and Princess of Havok freak out about it, jumping off booth seats and chairs, he just sits there. This'll be great; awesome music, cool bands, beautiful Tim Armstrong, new people... Unan looks at Princess of Havok, just as she looks at her. They must have the same idea.

"That's it!"

Dave gives them a ride to the club where the concert's going to be. He's not staying, though, because he has "something else" to do that night. He refuses to tell them what it is, though.

He drops them off at the door, three hours early. There are a few people there, already waiting in line. Princess of Havok and Unan seem to fit in quite well.

"Look, Unan. Our own kind," Havok comments, while stepping out of the car. She fixes her plaid pants with extra, useless zippers on the legs and reaches her hand out to help Unan.

"Yeah! Punk rock!" Unan is wearing ratty, old, men's dress pants and her red Rancid shirt. They say goodbye to Dave and take their place in line.

"I don't feel much like talking to these people," Havok whispers. She's fidgeting and messing with her new pyramid bracelet. Unan shrugs and turns to the guy next to her.

"Hey."

"Hi, what's up?" he replies.

"Ah, nothing. You on the guest list?" She can't really think of any small talk. What else do you say before a concert?

"Yeah." Unan's eyes open wide and her jaw drops. She turns to Havok.

"Now that's what *we* need. Can you imagine going backstage and meeting Rancid?!" she asks Havok. Princess of Havok thinks for a moment, picturing herself as a screaming, maniacal fan. No, that wouldn't do at all. She'd have to be cool and calm. Maybe say something like "hey, guys" and *then* jump on Tim Armstrong. That god of punk rock. Too bad he was married...

"We *will* get backstage, or my name isn't Princess of Havok," she replies. "I have a plan." Unan shakes her head.

"Oh boy," she says. Havok hopes there are cute roadies.

About three hours later, the line finally begins to move. Before either of them can say anything, a girl stops in front of them. She is wearing a plaid skirt, a thin white t-shirt, and boots. Her eyebrow, nose, lip, and ears are pierced; she is wearing a pyramid bracelet and bondage ring bracelet on one arm, a double pyramid on the other, and a spiked collar. She turns to them, smiling brightly.

"Hey, guys! Is this exciting or what?"

"Hell yeah!" Princess of Havok replies. Unan is ready to protest the intrusion, but she is interrupted, cut short by an apology from the girl.

"I'm really sorry about this. I hope you guys don't mind too much. See, I'm from a local fanzine in my area, and they're supposed to let me interview Rancid before the show," she explains. The line moves even closer to the door. "Those jerkoffs up ahead wouldn't let me in." They both keep their mouths shut. Once the girl is let in, she thanks them and rushes off.

Unan and Princess of Havok explore the inside of the club and head for the bathroom. Unan promised earlier to spike Havok's hair once they got in.

"That girl was pretty nice."

"Yeah. Awesome."

"At first, I thought she was going to be a –" Havok stops herself before muttering "punk slut," thinking of her plan. "I dunno. I just thought she wouldn't be good to mess with." People are moving in and out of the bathroom, toilets flushing, sinks running, while they just sit in the middle of it all.

"I know what you mean. Am I pulling your hair too hard?"

"Not at all."

When they're done, they split up. Princess of Havok tells Unan to go into the pit and wait for her there. She's a bit worried about her, but she has to go through with her plan. So Unan goes to wait, and Havok hangs around by the backstage door. She leans against the wall, trying to look good. Tons of guys pass by, but thinking of being with them makes her sick. Suddenly, a different guy walks past... is it Tim?!! It couldn't be, could it? No, wait, his lips are a bit different. She's just overly excited about being so close to the backstage area and starting to hallucinate.

"Hi," she says. He stops what he's doing and looks at her.

"Hey. You looking for someone?" he asks, scratching his arm. He's wearing a wifebeater. Somehow, he looks so innocent.

"No, actually..." She sighs. "I was just thinking about how great it would be to get backstage and meet Rancid."

"They're a great bunch of guys. Awesome, really." Something seems to click as he changes the expression on his face. "I... I could get you backstage. I mean, I think I could. I'm not a roadie or anything, but I work here," he explains, shrugging. He gives a quick glance behind him.

"Well, I'm here with a friend, and if you could do that for us...God!!! I don't know *what* I could possibly do to repay you," Havok replies, smiling. Music begins to play, and he looks behind him once more.

"I can't think of anything. You got something in mind?" She is taken aback by his answer, expecting him to be up front about it. But she knows what she has to do, what they all want.

"Maybe." She places a hand on his chest and lightly pushes him backstage and into the door of one of the rooms. They close it and lock it.

"What's your name?"

"Havok. And yours?"

"People call me Tim, but I go by Lint."

"Wow..." They mess around for a while, and Havok is quite sure she gets the go-ahead for a little meeting with Rancid. Unan will be *so* excited. She tries not to think too much about what she's doing. It's wrong, but... he's

80

nice, right? He's wonderful and he's so good-looking. Wait! She doesn't know a thing about him! This is fucked. Extremely fucked. As she contemplates what the hell she's doing there, the rhythm of a Less Than Jake song is pounded into her brain. But the smile plastered on her face, and the occasional sound or two that she makes causes Lint to think she's enjoying it. He continues, but almost hesitating. She doesn't seem, to him, like the kind of girl who would do something like this. He thought he wasn't the type of guy, either... he'd always had a fairly high respect for people. He would have let her backstage without this, but she seemed like she wanted it. He didn't even know how old she was. She could've been a kid. 'What the hell am I doing?' he thought. When they finish, Havok gives him a simple kiss on the cheek. He feels terrible... in fact, *sad* about what he's done to her. Before she can leave the room, he places a hand on her back.

"Again?" she whispers. Was that the rule? He immediately shakes his head.

"No, no. I... would you just take care of yourself? Please?" Lint pleads. Instead of waiting for an answer, he opens the door for her and leaves to prepare the stage for Rancid.

Unan is worried. Princess of Havok missed all of Less Than Jake, and she's still not back yet. When she finally comes back, Hepcat has started.

"Where were you?"

"Huh?"

"What took you so long?" Unan asks, frustrated.

"I was just wandering around." Unan doesn't believe her. Something is definitely not right. Before, she was bubbling with excitement, and now she's vacant. Blank.

"Your spikes are flat in the back."

"Oh?" Havok absent-mindedly places a hand on the back of her head. "Can you fix it?"

"Sure. C'mon, let's get back to the bathroom." Princess of Havok suddenly snaps back into reality.

"Shit! I forgot to tell him our names!!!" she cries. Unan is upset and confused. She grabs Princess of Havok by the arm and drags her along behind her.

"We're going right now, and I'm gonna fix your hair, and *you're* gonna tell me what the hell happened while you were gone!" she says.

While in the bathroom, again, they discuss everything. Unan is no longer angry with her sidekick, but she can't believe what she did. Princess of Havok tries her best to get over it, feeling in some way like she should have liked it more or played along better. He *was* good-looking, and he *had* been nice after all. Nicer than she expected. He didn't try to hurt her or treat her like shit, right? So many other people would have. But she forgives herself, and so does Unan. Things are okay.

Once they're back in the pit, Hepcat is almost done with their set. Unan and Princess of Havok dance together to a slower ska beat, giggling while they do. Most of the people seem fairly open-minded about it, but some move away. Damn homophobes. Two fat guys stand directly in front of them, blocking their view of the jumpy little singer onstage. They don't seem to notice who they've stepped in front of.

"Hey! What the hell do you think you're doing?!!" Princess of Havok cries. One of them turns around with his hands up, defensively.

"Don't worry! We're not staying long." He turns back around.

"Yeah, right, shithead," Unan mutters. Havok starts laughing. The guys must be about thirty or at least in their late twenties. Unan has a plan. Hepcat starts a new song. "Let's piss these guys off." They both begin to skank and make their way in front of the guys, squeezing in between them and other people.

"Lesbians."

"Assholes!!!" Havok yells, skanking violently. The guys begin to make fun of Hepcat, and Unan and Havok are ready to smack them.

"What the hell's your problem?" Unan asks.

"Yeah! If all you were gonna do is make fun of them, you didn't have to stand in front of us!" Havok's a bit angry. "Why did you even come here?!" They don't respond and just walk away. They have a feeling they'll be meeting them later.

Finally, the time has come. Rancid gets up on stage, and Unan starts jumping up and down.

"Yeah! Fuck yeah, baby!" she cries, pumping her fist into the air. "This is awesome!" Tim is wearing a black jacket and a black knit cap. Lars has a huge, orange and black mohawk. They can't quite see Brett behind everyone, and from their angle, Matt is positioned behind a speaker.

Quite a few songs into the set, Princess of Havok decides she needs to get a closer look at Tim Armstrong. She pushes her way into the center of the pit. Unan doesn't even notice until Havok is barely visible to her.

"Havok!" she yells over the music. People give her dirty looks, but she doesn't pay any attention to them. She sees those two guys from before making their way toward Princess of Havok.

Meanwhile, Havok is just doing anything that requires flailing her arms and legs around. Dancing to Tim's sweet voice and the ripping of chords. What better way to spend an evening? As she gets ready to move forward even more, she suddenly stops moving. Someone's holding onto her pants.

"Let go of me, jackass!" she yells, turning to see what's wrong. She sees the guys and assumes she's surrounded by their friends. The kind of guys who show up at just about *any* show to prove that they can kick ass in the mosh pit. Literally. Jocks with letter jackets, pseudo-punks wearing muscle shirts to show off their tan and what they accomplished at the gym... all there for one purpose. To beat up little punkies and punkettes and freaks that happened to be there.

"Look who it is! That little lesbian we saw before," one of the guys comments.

"Listen, fucker, I didn't ask for any shit! Why don't you just leave me alone?!" she cries. It's barely audible.

"No can do. We want to give you something you'll remember." For once, fear sets in. She takes a deep breath and hopes they don't find the conqueror later. Princess of Havok has no idea what they have in mind. Until they form a circle and begin pushing her roughly from one side to the other...

Unan keeps searching for her sidekick among the hundreds of people there. She thinks she catches a glimpse of her... She saw her before, but those guys stepped in front of her.

"Uh-oh," Unan mutters aloud, to herself. When she finally sees Havok, they're still pushing her around. With one violent thrust of the arms, she's down on the floor. "Fuck you! You bastards better leave her alone!" she yells. She can hear Princess of Havok's yells even from where she's standing. Unan tries to push her way through the crowd, but just ends up getting swept back to where she started. There's no possible way she could get to Havok before those guys kicked her ass.

Princess of Havok attempts to take another deep breath while she's down. Instead, she inhales blood and has to cough, spitting it back up onto her face. The floor smells of cigarettes and beer. She lifts her face only to see those jerks laughing. What wonderful people. One of them places a Doc Marten-clad foot near her, ready to kick her in the side. She moans, quietly, trying her best to get up, but soon feels a steel toe in her ribs.

"Ohhh... I hope to God you rot in hell," she whispers. And then... Lint appears out of nowhere, pushing through the guys, making his way toward her. He leans over.

"Havok? I thought I told you to take care of yourself! Oh well, it's okay. Grab on," he says, picking her up. She places a hand on his back and an arm around his neck, pressing her bloodied face to his chest. Unan sees Princess of Havok suddenly rise in the arms of some stranger. She's clinging to him; the circle has scattered, their job finished. Once Lint gets close enough to her, she runs toward him.

"Hey, that's my friend!"

"What's your name?" he asks, not stopping. She walks beside him.

"Unan."

"Unan..." Havok calls quietly, still holding on to Lint.

"Unan, we're gonna take Havok here to the hospital," he announces.

The lights are bright and blinding. Unan blinks, but when that doesn't work, she places a hand over her eyes.

"You alright?" Lint asks, turning around. He could feel her moving next to him. The waiting room is packed, so they're squashed together on one chair.

"Yeah, but... it's too..."

"Bright? Yeah, I know." She smiles as he puts a hand on Havok's shoulder. She's sitting in a wheelchair, attempting to sit up straight. "Don't worry. It shouldn't be too much longer. Try and keep your back up." Princess of Havok lets out a quiet moan. Unan pulls her knees up to her chin. "I'll be right back." Lint gets up and goes to the bathroom. She immediately takes his place on the chair.

"Havok? Is that the guy?"

"Yeah..." she groans.

"Wow! Are you feeling okay? Can I get you anything?" Unan is spazzing. She feels bad for not having been able to help at the concert.

"I'm fine." They wait until Lint returns. He comes back with a wet paper towel. Unan gets ready to move and give him his seat back.

"It's okay. You can have the chair," he offers. He kneels on the ground and starts cleaning Princess of Havok's face, wiping off dried blood. His wifebeater is stained with it, but he doesn't seem to care too much. Lint looks worried; a solitary wrinkle graces his furrowed brow. "Hold your head up." He holds her chin with his hand. "Just tell me if I'm hurting you."

"No, you're not. I think I'm alright."

Once they finish their visit at the hospital, Lint drives Unan and Princess of Havok home – to the coffeehouse for now. The nurse told them that their friend was lucky; nothing was broken, amazingly enough. All she needed was to get some rest and heal because she would probably be sore for at least a couple days. When Unan goes to call Dave and tell him what happened, Havok invites Lint to stay for a bit.

"I don't know..." he replies, still standing. He had even carried her in and laid her down on the couch.

"But you've done so much for me. Please?"

"I guess I could. As long as I call and let them know I won't be back tonight," he says, thinking.

"Okay. I mean... that was just... you were really nice to me. And I don't understand why you care so much. Not that I'm not grateful. I am. I wasn't expecting that, though," Princess of Havok explains. He moves her legs gently so he can sit down on the couch.

"Do you mind?"

"Not at all." Once he's seated, she lays her legs on his lap. He absent-mindedly begins to rub her feet.

"I care because... well, I'm not really sure. When we both went into the back room, all I could think about was what you were about to do. And when it was happening, all these questions were flying through my head. How old is she? *Who* is she? What's she like? Is she really the kind of girl to do this? I thought it was what you wanted, but I don't think I made it clear that you didn't have to. And when it was over, I felt terrible. I knew I should have stopped it and not let it go where it did. I thought I needed to do something to make it up to you. So... I'm not a stalker or anything, but I was keeping track of you. Just to make sure you were alright. I don't know... I just had this really bad feeling." Lint stares off into space, almost seeming to contemplate something. Unan steps out, holding a Surge bottle.

"I see you guys made yourselves comfortable," she comments. She sits on the floor, cross-legged.

"Shit, I'm really sorry about getting your shirt dirty," Princess of Havok apologizes. He shrugs and stretches his legs.

"It's no problem. I've got tons more. Besides, as long as you're okay, and I was able to help, then nothing else matters," he replies.

"Dave's coming over," Unan interrupts, happily.

Dave doesn't *seem* angry when he arrives at the coffeehouse. But he isn't overjoyed, either. He glares at Lint from the moment he walks in the door.

"What the fuck happened to Havok?" he demands.

"Dave..."

"No, I want him to tell me what went on."

"She got beat up," Lint says, sensing there's something wrong.

86

"Dave, he saved her," Unan announces.

"Oh!" He seems to think about it for a moment, and then holds his hand out to him. "I'm Dave."

"Lint," he responds, shaking Dave's hand. "They call me Lint."

Lint, born William Timothy Randall, grew up in a city just next to Canton. He became a Rancid fan at a young age, learning of the joys of punk rock from his older sister. She called him Little Lint, thus his nickname formed. Still, others refused to call him that, so he went by Tim. He continued telling his story.

"When I was sixteen, my sister died. She was going back to her car or something at night, during work, and some guy just started beating her up. She didn't even have a lot of money. They found her and took her to the hospital where she passed away later. She... she was real fragile. My parents went crazy. *Seriously* crazy. My mom was shipped off to some asylum, and I have no idea where my dad is now. So when I found work at the club, I went for it. They have some awesome shows. Besides, I've decided that I'd like to grow up in a way that would have made my sister proud," he explains.

"How old are you?" Unan asks, quietly.

"Nineteen."

"Groovie... skavoovie... good night," Havok mutters, already half-asleep. Her eyelids flutter and Unan giggles; her hair looks funny smashed up against the couch.

"I better get going now. There's this... well, I just gotta go," Dave announces, hurriedly. "It was nice meeting you."

"Yeah, you too." Dave rushes out the door, and Lint shrugs. "I don't know how well *that* went."

"Dave's been a little weird lately. Give him some time," Unan replies, standing up and stretching. She looks at the clock and begins to pace back and forth, back and forth. She's confused as to whether or not she should ask him to stay. Before she can say anything, Lint speaks up.

"Is it alright if I stay here? I mean... I might wake her up if I try to move, and she needs to get her rest."

"Yeah! That's fine. Do you want anyone, I mean... any*thing*?" Unan nearly slaps herself for that one, but realizes it's okay when Lint begins to laugh. He has a pretty smile.

"Thanks, but I'm fine."

"Well, if you need anything later, just call me or something. I'll be on the other side of the counter," she offers.

"Okay." She begins to walk away. When she's far enough away to be out of his sight – but close enough to see them – she turns around. Unan watches as Lint messes with Havok's pants, straightening them out and playing with the extra zippers. He smiles at her almost death-still body and fixes her shirt, which had been riding up her back. When all is well, he leans his head against the couch and looks at her with caring, delicate brown-green eyes. His eyelids slowly fall shut, and Unan is happy.

The next morning, Unan wakes up in time to see Lint sneaking out the door. She runs out after him, making sure her boxers don't fly off.

"Shit," she mutters. "Shit!" She catches up to him in the street. "Hey! Where the hell are you going?! After you... after you did *that* to her and then after being so nice? Are you leaving just like that?! You can't! Can't you at least wait until she wakes up and says goodbye?" Lint turns around slowly. He's still wearing the bloody shirt, and Unan cringes.

"I'm not leaving. Well, not permanently. I just have to let the people at work know why I was gone yesterday," he explains. "Seriously, I wanna see her again. I'd love to see her again," he says, smiling from ear to ear. "I left her a note. Don't worry about it. But right now, I *really* gotta haul ass." Lint rushes off to his car. Unan trudges back into the coffeehouse, yawning. Havok is sitting up now, apparently reading her letter.

"He wants to see me again," she announces, looking up at Unan from the couch, her eyes shining brightly.

"How are you feeling?"

"Better! Well, still a little sore. Do you believe that?!"

"Yeah, you got thrown around pretty hard..."

"No, silly! That he wants to see me again!"

"I guess so... how do you think purple would look on my hair?" Unan asks, striking a pose. Havok giggles.

"Gorgeous, dahling!" She pauses for a moment. "Are you angry with me about what I did yesterday?"

"No! I mean... well, maybe a little. It was so... sudden. And he's so beautiful. I mean, not that *that* means everything. And... I sorta wish I could've done the same."

"No, you don't. *Believe me,* it wasn't fun. Well... no, it wasn't fun," Havok replies, shaking her head.

"I didn't mean in *that* situation. I mean, somewhere else at a different time. With Dave," Unan explains. She laughs and puts an evil grin on her excited face. "Cuz he's delicious."

"Unan! Hehe. What's up with Dave anyway? He's acting kinda funny."

"I don't know. But he's beautiful."

"Unan—"

"Beautiful."

"Unan-"

"Beautiful."

"Unan!" Havok cries. "What's gotten into you, you little hornball?!" Unan giggles... then laughs... then cackles, so much that she falls to the floor. Havok shakes her head. "Call him up, Silly Girl!" Unan stops, then grins.

"Me a silly, silly girl!"

The day begins nicely and then turns into one large thunderstorm that seems to hover over their town. It's alright, though, because then they don't have as many customers at the coffeehouse, and they can talk and listen to whatever they want. Dave should be stopping by later.

"Truth or dare?" Unan asks.

"C'mon! You already know everything about me!"

"Pick."

"Truth." The conqueror thinks for a moment while her sidekick sips on cappuccino. "Well?"

"Did you do it with Sexy Alexey?"

"I didn't stay over there for nothing." Havok's eyes sparkle, and Unan giggles.

"Okay."

"Can we put in Fiona?"

"Sure." The day is a bit mellow, so they go with the theme. After Havok starts the tape, she sits back down.

"Alexey liked her. He said there was this one part that reminded him of me—" Suddenly, the door is flung open, and a familiar face steps in.

"Lint!" Havok cries, jumping up and running to hug him, forgetting about her sore side.

"Hey, there. Hi, Unan," he calls out, muffled because he has his face buried in Havok's shoulder. She simply waves and smiles. "I'm glad to see you again."

"Yeah... will you come sit down and join us?"

After Lint's been there for a while, Unan decides to call Dave again to see why he's not there yet. Nobody answers the phone. She wonders what the hell is going on. First, he doesn't go to the Rancid concert with them. Then, he's angry – or was he? – about Lint. Then he just leaves. And now, he said he'd be over, but he's not. And nobody even answers the phone at his house.

"Dammit!" Unan yells. She stomps back over to where Lint and Princess of Havok are. "I don't *get* this!" As they're all waiting there, Dave storms in from the rain.

"I've made my decision!"

"What?" Unan asks. They're all confused.

"MAKE ME PUNK!"

The sun's not shining. Nevertheless, the war still goes on.

| Dave's Transition

They are all silent for a few minutes. Then, Unan's face lights up.

"Punk fuckin' rock! Alright!" she cries, running over to him happily and giving him a hug. She nearly knocks him over. Havok gives him a hug, too, saying that it should be fun.

"Hey, man, nobody can make you punk. You already are. You've got spirit, and you don't seem like anyone else I know," Lint announces.

"I guess you're right. Thanks. I'm just ready for a change. I dunno. Not make me punk, but maybe help me look different. I'm kinda bored with all the black!" Dave replies.

Instead of working on it that day, they just chill for a while. The next day, Havok takes a little trip to Lint's house, but she tells Unan she's just going for a walk. On her way there, she observes how empty the streets of suburbia have become. Everyone must be on vacation, driving their expensive little cars. When she arrives, she knocks lightly on the door.

"Hey! Come on in. I wasn't expecting you so early," Lint says.

Obviously, because he's only wearing a pair of boxers... how heavenly.

"I'm sorry. I hope I didn't wake you up or anything."

"No, it's alright." She enters the small, white house. Standing at the door, she finds herself facing a hallway. On the left is the living room, and to her right, what seems to be a kitchen and small dining room. Down the hallway, there are three more rooms. Probably bedrooms. She doesn't remember if she saw basement windows from outside or not—

"You can sit down. I have to go throw some clothes on anyway." As Lint travels to the end of the hallway, Princess of Havok lays down on a couch. It's very comfortable, and she wonders how much it cost. She messes around with a safety pin on her cargo pants as The Germs start to play in the bedroom.

When Lint finally emerges from the hallway, which is only about five minutes later, Havok has the TV turned on.

"Heh, kill your TV. I don't know why I keep it around anyway. I hardly ever watch it," he mutters. She turns it off and looks at him. His mohawk is spikier than ever, and his pants! What a cute little old-skooler.

"Should we call Dave first or just drop by there?" she asks, her eyes focusing on his bright green hair.

"He told me we could just drop by." They had planned to make Dave over and bring him back to the coffeehouse to surprise Unan. They walk out to the car...

"Whoa! Wait a minute. This isn't the car you were driving the other night," Havok announces. She motions toward the beautiful, royal blue Thunderbird parked there.

"No, it isn't. I was borrowing one from this guy at work. I picked my baby up from the shop last night." Havok runs a hand over the door.

"It's wonderful."

On the way to Dave's, they listen to a band called Lit. Lint suggests they go see them play sometime. They pick up Dave and go to Target to look for some clothes. Havok says she has something simple planned out. Something that will do for now, so when Dave gets used to them, he'll be able to start looking on his own for what strikes him. After buying what they need, they return to Lint's place so Dave can change. As Lint and Havok admire their work of art, he speaks up.

"Hey, you think you could do my eyebrow?"

"What?!" Havok cries.

"Really. I've always wanted to, but I didn't get a chance yet. How about now?" Dave asks, his eyes lighting up.

"I can't be here for this," Havok says, returning to the living room. Lint goes and gathers what he'll need to pierce Dave's eyebrow.

When they are completely finished, they go back to the coffeehouse. Unan has been wondering what's up all day. They – Lint and Havok – make her stand in front of the doorway with her eyes closed. Before she gets her surprise, Havok pats her on the head, careful not to flatten her newly purple spikes.

"You're gonna love this," she whispers, excitedly. After Unan is told to open her eyes, she is faced with a wonderful sight. Dave is standing there in all his delicious beauty. Gorgeously formed, spiked, black hair. The usual, but much more defined now. His eyebrow is pierced! Blue eyes shining happily. A striped shirt graces the top half of his body. Cargo shorts. Cute little boys' socks. Vans. Unan's jaw has dropped.

"Dave! You look so... *different*! I love it! This has to be one of the best surprises I've ever gotten!"

"Am I good different?"

"Absolutely! You look different from before, but somehow, like *you*. This is so *groovie*!" They all laugh at Unan's reaction. "Dave, I love you!"

"I love you too, silly." He walks over and gives her a big hug, kissing her ear. "You'll always be my silly girl," he whispers. It drives her up the wall, and she has to try hard to contain herself.

"Well, what should we do now?" Unan asks. "I feel like going out somewhere and just hanging out. Fucking around."

"I was just telling Havok that we should go down to Plymouth. If we could go to Repeat the Beat, I could get us tickets to go see Lit. I'm not

93

working that night, and I was hoping we could all hang out. I... I think you guys are awesome, and if I could be your friend—" He starts to blush.

"Aw, Lint, of course you can!"

"I think he's right. We should go to Plymouth. I love it there," Dave announces.

It seems as though Plymouth is more populated right now. The fountain is going and people are everywhere. It's still only mid-afternoon, so the streetlights aren't on yet. They are walking along quietly after having exited Lint's car, and Havok feels a hand slip over hers. Not understanding, she quickly looks down to see whose it is. Lint turns toward her, giving her a half-smile.

"I hope you don't mind. It's... been a while..." He looks like a little child pleading for a toy. "I don't really have any friends," he confesses.

"It's alright," she responds, grinning. She is confused about what she's feeling, but it sure is nice to have someone close.

After buying tickets, they mess around by the fountain. People who were previously sitting on the side get up and move over to the benches surrounding it. Dave scoops up a large handful of water and throws it at Unan.

"Hey! Get back here, geek boy," she mutters, chasing after him. He screams like a little girl and flails his arms.

"Eek! Eek!" Dave cries, giggling. Unan stops, momentarily, to notice that Lint and Havok seem to be in their own world. Dave runs into her, hugging her from behind, nearly disturbing her balance.

"Look. I think they're really getting along well," she comments, pointing at them. They're just talking at first, but then they both stand up and start pushing each other playfully.

"Yeah. I guess so." He blows on her neck and kisses it, running away quickly.

"Stop!" She smiles, slowly running a hand down the length of her neck. "Delicious boy." She waits for a second and then chases after him. Meanwhile, Lint and Havok are running around the fountain side. Havok is attempting not to fall in, but Lint is trying to push her. They both stop and turn toward each other.

"Don't even push me in there," Princess of Havok says, holding her hands up in defense.

"Fine, I won't. No problem."

"That's good," she replies, shoving him over to the side. Unexpectedly, he falls back, right into the water. She'd thought he would be a little sturdier. But it was more like he *wanted* to get wet. "I'm so sorry, Lint!" she cries when he resurfaces.

"You molester! Get away from me!" he laughs. He must have had a super-hawk because it had not fallen down yet, even in the water. Havok makes a mental note to ask him exactly what he used.

"Very funny..." she replies, walking slowly along the edge.

"Don't think you're gonna get away *that* easily!" he says. His cold, wet hand grabs her ankle and pulls her in. After she splashes a bit, she giggles.

"You're crazy." They both stand up in the water. "You nut." His plain white t-shirt is clinging to his skin. He makes a face and strips it off, throwing it out onto the sidewalk. She places her hands onto his chest and begins to kiss him. Her emotions are still confusing... she's only recently met him, but right now that doesn't matter. What happened at the concert is the furthest thing from her mind. Unan and Dave arrive at the scene.

"Woo-hoo! Sexy water fight! *More! More!*" Unan yells, pumping her fist into the air a few times. She jumps up and down, dancing around like a little fairy.

"Shit. You can't do anything fun without some asshole fucking things up..." Dave mutters, under his breath. Unan turns to see why he's so angry all of a sudden. A police car is pulling up, but nobody gets out. The window is rolled down, and a plump officer sticks his head out.

"What the hell are you kids doing in there?! Get out, *right now*! I better not see you screwing around in there again while *I'm* around, or I'll personally find all you delinquents a new home at the county jail. God, you'd think they'd have the common decency to be a little quieter," he says, loudly, to himself. They walk over to the very edge of the park. They stand, unmoving. Lint fishes a wet cigarette out of his pocket and attempts to light it. The policeman pulls out a sweet treat from plastic packaging.

"*Popo with a hoho*!!!" Unan yells. Dave and Havok expected something like that to come from her mouth, so they were ready to start sprinting back to Lint's T-bird. But he is a little confused when it happens. A couple seconds later, he runs to follow them.

"Hey! Wait up!" When they are all back at the car, they hop in and take off. That night, everyone goes home. And Princess of Havok actually finds her way back to her parental units for the first time in about three weeks or so. Unan attempts to settle in at the coffeehouse all by herself. It's been a while since she was there alone.

In the middle of the night, she is still trying to get comfortable in the heat. She hears rustling around outside. Only one thing comes to mind.

"Please don't be Ryan, please don't be Ryan, please don't be Ryan..." she whispers, quietly. She wonders what she'd do if it *was* him. The door opens, slightly creaking. Unan knows she didn't leave it unlocked this time, or she thinks so at least. She'd forgotten a couple times before, but luckily nobody found out about the missing money. But this meant that the only possible person it could be was...

"Havok?" Unan calls out in the darkness. She hears a few footsteps.

"I'm sorry. Did I wake you up?"

"No. Come here." Unan gets up to turn on a small light.

"No. Unan, you don't have to turn on the—" Havok hears a click. "Light. Okay, nevermind." Her eyes are dull, and her hair is smashed against her head on one side. Her hands are shaking. "Please, don't... don't say anything. I just have to—" Unan throws her arms around her sidekick, trying to get a better look. Havok's lip is split, and there's a large bump on her forehead. It seems as though her eye is slightly black, but she can't tell if it's just the lighting.

"What the hell happened?! Who did this?"

"Who do you think? I... at home... fuck it. I'm not going back there, I'm not!" Havok sobs, burying herself into Unan's shoulder. "I'd rather die."

"Stop it! Don't say that again. I don't want you to die. And you don't have to go back there if you don't want to. You don't belong with people who don't respect you."

"I'm... I'm permanently kicked out of the house. I mean, they're not kidding either. I still have to go to school and shit. They made it pretty clear that they don't want any trouble with the state."

"That's fucked. But maybe it'll be better this way," Unan suggests, trying to make the best out of everything.

"It just pisses me off that they *pretend* to care so much, and then they do this to me."

"So what did you do with all your stuff? Did you walk here?"

"No. My shit's out in the car. I'm moving in with Lint." Unan doesn't know what to think. He seems trustworthy and everything, but people can change. And why didn't Havok call her and ask to move in with *her*? Unan lets her go.

"Oh."

"Please don't make that face. I'll actually be even closer now. It'll be just like I live here. Like usual!" Unan is tempted to ask why she *doesn't* just live there, but she decides not to. She keeps quiet and tries to be happy for her faithful sidekick. Why shouldn't she be? After all, like she said, she *will* be closer.

"Okay. That's good."

"Well, I'm gonna get going now. I just wanted to drop by and tell you what's going on. I'll see you tomorrow." Havok turns to leave.

"Havok?"

"Yeah?"

"Be careful."

"Don't worry about me, Unan. I got it under control." Unan isn't so sure about that. Especially after seeing her like this. She can't help but worry.

The next day, Unan goes to visit Havok at her new home. But when she gets there, she doesn't ring the doorbell. She first snoops around, investigating. It's a plain, white house, seemingly tiny from the outside. There's no garage. Dandelions infest the grass, which looks like Lint once tried to take care of it but gave up. She glances at the car; it really *is* a nice car... She finally walks up the steps and rings the doorbell.

"Hey!" Lint greets her after opening the front door. "How are you?"

"Good. It's a nice morning," Unan blurts. It's too bad the sky is gray, dotted with rain clouds. She just couldn't think of anything to say after having just been searching around his house for a reason Havok shouldn't stay there.

"Um, yeah," he replies. "If you like dull weather."

"Is Havok around?"

"Yeah, but she's sleeping right now. I told her she needed to get some rest after that shit last night." Okay, Unan thought. Controlling... "Would you like to come in?"

"Sure." She notices a few pillows on the couch. "I thought she was sleeping."

"What? Oh, that. I slept out here. She's using my bed. I figured it was the least I could do." Unan sighs. Maybe she's wrong. There's no problem with Havok moving in to Lint's house. "You know, I can't tell you not to worry. You're her best friend, and I understand that. But I swear to you, I'm gonna try to take care of her the best I can. Maybe you won't believe me when I say this, but I *really* care about her, and I don't want to see her hurt," Lint explains.

"And you're not just saying that because you fucked her, right?" Unan asks.

"Jesus! No! I... I still don't even know what possessed me to do that. I'd like to start all over again with her. But I can't pretend that none of that happened, because it did. And we all know that," he replies, sitting down on a chair. "But I know when I meet someone special. And I can tell when they're sincere about what they say. You guys and Dave seem to be, and I'd really appreciate it if you and Dave could forgive me for what I did to her," Lint announces. He is looking down at the floor.

"I do. I'm sorry about what I said. It's just all... so sudden. One of our best friends recently moved away. Now Dave wants to be all different. Everything's changing so fast that I can't handle it," Unan apologizes. She stands up and peeks down the hallway while Lint isn't looking. She sees a blanket moving in the bedroom and sits back down, quickly. Havok comes out a couple seconds later, eyes scrunched, dragging a sheet behind her.

"It's so bright in here," she says, still groggy. It really wasn't, but the shades in the bedroom had been drawn, so it was a strain on her eyes. Lint immediately stands up, hearing her voice – because he hadn't been looking – and helps her over to the couch.

"You need to get more sleep than that," he tells her.

"Oh! Hi, Unan," she says, seeing her there already. "What are you talking about? I'm fine. I'm awake," she says, waving his hands away.

"For now. You're gonna be smashed tomorrow," he comments. He runs a hand over his mohawk. Havok leans back and lays on Unan's lap.

"Such a lovely day," she mutters.

"A week until Lit," Lint says, smiling. Only moments later, Havok is snoring lightly.

The days pass by like seconds, and it's finally time for the awaited concert. Lint offers to drive them all, and they gladly accept. So when the time comes, they pile into the T-bird and drive to the club. When they walk in, Havok is shaking a little, and Unan decides to hold her hand.

"You'll be fine," she whispers.

"I know. I'm just a wimpy punk," Havok replies, half-smiling.

"I wish I had a banana." Dave overhears her and comes over, laughing. He puts an arm around Unan.

"I have a banana."

"Well, where is it?!" she asks, confused. He grins.

"I can't take it out in public. I might get arrested."

"Gross!" Unan slaps him, lightly, and Havok giggles.

This time, they are content to just stay outside of the mosh pit, on the side of the club. Dave and Unan play around while Lint and Havok kinda hold each other and talk before the concert. When Havok makes a quick trip to the bathroom, Lint walks over.

"What can I do to keep her in one place?" he asks Unan, quietly. He's fidgeting a little, balling his hands into fists and then relaxing them rhythmically.

"What do you mean?" Dave says.

"Well, I know she's not gonna be able to stand still later, and she's probably going to want to hop right in the middle of everything. She's already got more energy than before, but I'm not so sure about her getting in here," he explains.

"Carry her," Unan jokes. Lint seems to be thinking about it for a couple minutes.

"I think I just might."

The opening band is some local band, which they don't really care for, so they pretty much just stand around. When Lit finally comes on, Lint is carrying Havok on his shoulders. The concert seems to fly by. At the end, the singer is the only one left on the stage, and he's messing with his zipper.

"Take off your pants!" Havok yells loudly, pumping her fist into the air. He lets them drop enough to reveal light blue boxers, but then pulls them back up and on. Instead of getting to see his body south of the border, they see his chest as he pulls off his shirt and throws it into the crowd. Soon after, he walks off the stage, and the lights turn on.

"I think *you* should do that," Unan says to Dave with a straight, serious face.

"Not for all these people."

"Oh, but why not?"

"That's strictly for a silly girl."

They are ready to leave, but Lint stops them and tells them that the real trick is to stay after for a while so you get to eventually meet the band. They go out for something to eat and come back later. When they do, the guitarist and bass player are outside on the steps. Apparently, the singer and drummer had something else to take care of.

"Ohmygod! It's Lit!" Havok says. "Well, half." They laugh.

"Were you guys at the show tonight?" bass guy asks.

"Yeah. It was fuckin' awesome," Lint replies, speaking for them all.

"Have a seat. Stay a while. We'd love to chat," guitar guy offers. "We've got a day between shows, so we probably won't head out until early afternoon tomorrow." They both seem like really down-to-earth guys.

"Okay!" Unan cries, sitting on the bassist's lap right away.

"Unan!" Dave protests. He's not really embarrassed... just surprised. But the bass player just laughs.

"It's alright. Don't worry about it." He places a hand on her leg. "What's your name?" he asks her.

"Unan."

"Really?"

"Well... no. But I don't think I remember my real name."

"And the rest?"

"Well, that's Del—Dave, I mean. And then there's Princess of Havok and Lint," Unan introduces them all. The guitarist nods and says hi to all of them.

"I think I remember you guys."

"They were the ones standing off to the side. And Havok, here, was on his shoulders yelling for your brother to strip," bass guy says, smiling. They continue to talk for a while, just hanging out. Unan decides to be a bit daring.

"Do you have a marker or something?" she asks them. They look as though they were expecting that sooner or later.

"Actually, yeah. Where do you want me to sign? Got any paper?"

"Shit, no." She thinks for a moment, and then lifts up her shirt. "But you can sign my chest!" she cries, excitedly. She is proud of herself for thinking of it.

"Whoa! Okay," bass guy agrees.

"Can I sign you, too?" guitar guy asks, and Unan nods, standing up. Dave, Havok, and Lint are laughing. It's great that these guys are so nice and friendly. As they're signing, the lead singer from the local band steps outside, followed by the frumpy, cocky bassist.

"You call that entertainment?" he says, smirking at the scene outside the club. The guys from Lit glare at him, obviously pissed.

"Yeah, I do. I love getting to know the people who like our music and appreciate it. What do *you* enjoy?" guitar guy asks. Unan frowns at the local bassist, who is walking toward the bus.

"We are going to enjoy these beautiful females," the local singer responds, nodding toward the side of the bus. They look; two girls are standing there, scantily clad. Lousy, dirty girls who give their gender a bad name and only come to concerts to say they screwed the band.

"Disgusting," Havok mutters. "You don't even know their names."

"Yeah. And they'll love you tonight, pretending to like your music, long enough for you to take advantage of them. But it's the other way around. And tomorrow night, they'll love whoever else is playing at the club," Lint explains, his eyes centered on the singer. "I've seen it a million times, and I think it's ridiculous."

"Fine for you. But I don't get my rocks off signing the flat chest of some sickly-looking girl," the local bassist comments, entering the bus. Unan closes her eyes. It wasn't *her* fault she had some type of metabolism problem. And she ate. She apparently just didn't hold it in. What a bastard...

"I'm so glad we don't have to share a bus with you jerkoffs," bass guy announces.

"Yeah, it *is* good because you wouldn't have anywhere to sleep tonight. We'll be busy entertaining," the local singer says, closing the door behind him with a mischievous smile on his face. The bass player looks at Unan, who's standing there, frozen, with her shirt still up. He finishes signing her chest and hands the marker to the guitarist. As he finishes, the bass player gives Unan a light kiss on the cheek.

"Don't listen to them, sweetie. I think you guys are awesome. And I really hate assholes like that. I want you guys to keep up what you're doing.

You gotta be strong to be yourself and stay that way." Wonderful words of advice. They listen and agree, vowing to never give up hope in their struggle. The guys proceed to give both Havok and Unan kisses and to shake hands with Dave and Lint. They promise to visit if they're ever in the state again, as long as Unan gives them the address of the coffeehouse.

Another memory never to be forgotten. The sun continues to shine, and the war goes on.

| A Pickle in the Night

The time has come yet again to go back to school. It does bring to mind the fact that one of them is gone. But they attempt to forget. This year, they will be juniors, but it makes no difference. They will still have to face the threat of conformity and battles to come.

Unan walks to Lint's house to pick up Havok on the first day of school. It's strange to see so many people back in town for the fall. As she's nearing the house, she spots them sitting on the steps, just talking.

"Hey!" she calls out, waving.

"Hi!" Havok cries, flying down the sidewalk to greet her. She's wearing her old outfit again. Boots, striped socks, skirt, white blouse... no sweater vest because of the heat. Lint's just hanging out, wearing cargo shorts and no shirt. Unan thinks it's a shame they have to wear shirts in school. She'd like to see Dave walk down the hallway like that. Havok gives her a hug and then grabs her hand, leading her toward the house.

"Hey, Unan. Sup?" Lint asks.

"Not much. Just hot."

"Since I'm not working today, do you guys want a ride? I mean, at least the car's got air-conditioning," he offers, shrugging. They gladly accept. Lint runs inside to get some shoes on – old Converses – and they're off.

Once at school, they say goodbye to their friend. Havok gives Lint a quick peck on the cheek and rushes out, letting Unan out of the backseat. They soon meet up with Dave. He looks like a Salvation Army model with his new clothes. Once he sees them, he comes over and gives them both hugs. Unan finds it humorous because her back is sweaty, and when Dave lets go of her, her shirt is sticking to her.

In school, everyone is being told to go to their old homerooms from last year. Except the freshmen, who pile into the gym. So Dave and Unan leave Havok to go to another wing of the school. She begins skipping, excited about all the adventures they'll have that year. Once she reaches the room, though, her mood changes. Havok sits down at a desk in the corner, props her leg up on it, and resumes her habit of picking her nails with a pocketknife.

"Ewww... there's that girl from last year. The one that hung out with that gay guy. Right over there!" a prep whispers to another. She looks up for a moment. Just long enough to respond.

"No, it wasn't me. She's my twin."

"Really?!" Havok rolls her eyes and watches the teacher as she saunters in.

"Okay, we're just going to do a roll call," she announces. When they are almost finished, a little chica scurries into the room.

"Yeah, I'm late. I know. Bite me," she says, taking a spot near Havok. Her knee-high boots are visible behind the slits in her black skirt. She is wearing a skimpy blue top.

"What's your name?" the teacher snaps, not laughing.

"Veda Guillen." Princess of Havok is unsure of what to think of her. She *seems* to be pretty groovie. Havok can't tell if she's dressed for the heat or dressed to show herself off. She makes a mental note to tell Unan and Dave when she sees them. She continues eyeing the little chica as she carves an anarchy symbol into the desk. A few silent, awkward minutes go by with the rest of the classroom staring at Veda. She glances at the clock, quickly.

"Are we finished yet? I'm about due for another quick fix," she announces, leaving the room.

Half an hour before it is time, Princess of Havok walks out into the hallway, only to find Unan already wandering absent-mindedly. She runs up behind her and jumps on her back, wrapping her legs around Unan's waist. Unan giggles and gallops around.

"See anyone interesting?"

"No. You?"

"Some chick named Veda. She had cool boots," Havok replies, climbing off Unan's back. Unan pats her on the head as Dave approaches them.

"Prep stompers?" she asks, a twinkle in her eye.

"I don't know."

"Howdy, girls," Dave interrupts. "Let's go outside."

It's boiling out, but they're more interested in observing everyone. They see Veda sitting on the concrete steps just outside the school. She has her legs apart, and her skirt hangs between them, showing off her almost hooker-ish boots.

"Wow, she's smokin' a cigar," Unan says, almost a little too loudly. They all watch as half the school's population of boys attempts to flirt with her as they leave. One particularly cocky jock sits right down next to her.

"Hey, baby," he says, trying to sound smooth and sexy. She blows smoke in his face.

"Hey, jockstrap. You mind moving? You're blocking my view," she declares. Instead of listening, he tries to continue the conversation.

"That's a real nice skirt you've got there." He begins to run a finger up and down her leg. Veda pulls the cigar out of her mouth. "But—"

"It would look even better on your floor, right?" she asks, breathily.

"I was just thinking that..."

"And then you woke up. Get a life, cheesedick," Veda replies, flicking ashes onto his jeans. She quickly throws the cigar back into her mouth and puts her legs together, throwing her skirt over them and shaking her head. Havok giggles, finding the situation quite humorous. She leaves Dave and Unan – conversing amongst each other – to sit next to Veda.

"Hey," she says, trying to be friendly. Veda sighs and hangs her arm over her knee.

"Don't tell me *you* want some of this, too..." she groans, flashing her leg. Princess of Havok takes a few minutes to grasp what she said.

"Oh... you mean... me? No," she stammers, sheepishly.

"Don't be surprised. I've had offers," Veda remarks, laughing. She flicks the cigar remains down the steps and holds her head in her hands. Red highlights shine forth from behind her black hair.

"I wouldn't doubt it. I mean, I know how it is. I just wanted to say I saw you handle that guy back there. It was hella groovie." Havok glances at her, almost in reverence, as if she has finally found someone who knows what it feels like to be *that* girl.

"Yeah. You get used to it after a while."

"Trust me. I know." They sit in silence for a few moments. Dave and Unan are ready to walk back home with their friend.

"Before you leave... Well, I didn't catch your name," Veda announces, putting a hand up to her face to block the sun.

"Just call me Havok," she giggles, running to Unan's side. "And you're Veda, right?"

"Yup. Veda Guillen. See you around," she announces, looking off into the distance. Unan, Dave, and Havok start toward the coffeehouse.

"Yeah. Watch out for preps. I've seen too many go flying down these front steps in the past," Havok calls behind her.

About halfway home, Princess of Havok attempts to think up a topic of conversation. Unan is picking a dandelion apart, piece-by-piece, letting the yellow petals take to air like insects. Dave simply watches her as they walk back, sweaty and quiet. The humidity sucks any extra strength out of them, throwing them into exhaustion and boredom.

"So, what did you think about her?" Princess of Havok asks.

"Cool." Unan ruffles her own spikes and tosses the dandelion stem into oblivion. Dave nods, tapping a rhythm on his legs with his large palms. Havok is unable to distinguish whether they are just too hot to care or if she made a bad judgment call. She takes it to be the latter. She thought they were similar, but maybe Veda was just slutty like the others. But who was to say then that Havok wasn't a slut as well?

Unan and Dave drop Princess of Havok off at Lint's house. They both say they are busy, but the truth comes out later that evening. Unan is lying on the couch, and Dave puts Marvelous 3 into the CD player.

"Blah blah blah," she says, loudly. Dave sits on the floor next to her.

"What are you doing?" he asks, confused.

"Blah-blah blah blah," she responds.

"Wha—I don't get it." He shakes his head.

"I'm doing an impression of Havok. Pretty good, huh?"

"I've never seen you so bitter before. What's wrong, conqueror?" Dave questions, tickling her feet. She squirms and giggles, her purple hair still spiked from earlier.

"I don't want to hear any more about Veda or whoever. Who cares anyway? I have all the friends I want and need already." Unan crosses her arms over her chest and pouts like a child. "And her boots were *not* prep stompers."

"You really don't think so?" he asks.

"Absolutely not. They're only good for standing on street corners, waiting for a quick twenty-five cents," she explains, staring across the coffeehouse. She'd have to remember to turn the air up higher.

"Is that all it is now?" Dave jokes. Unan frowns.

"Not funny."

"I'm only kidding, Unan! Maybe we shouldn't be so hard on her. We haven't even met her. Then we'd be the way everyone is with us." She thinks for a moment, sitting up and taking a deep breath.

"Okay, fine."

"Now, come here!" Dave says, pulling her towards him.

That night, Havok leaves the safety of Lint's arms, nearly tripping over the fan as she walks out of the bedroom. It was just a silly craving for a pickle, that's all. A stupid little pickle. So why did she feel so weird about it? She opens the refrigerator door and stares blankly at the perfect amount of food they manage to sustain. She slaps her leg where it feels as though a spider may have been crawling. After thinking about it, she grabs a pickle and sits on the couch. Havok turns the TV on and entertains herself by using the search button to make the channels continually flip from one to another. When she's nearly finished, she hears Lint get out of bed and start down the hallway. She crams the last quarter of the pickle into her mouth, letting the sour juice from it crawl down her throat before swallowing it.

"What are you doing out here?" Lint asks, startling her. He rubs his eyes, which look more brown than green in the dim light.

"Uh, nothing! Just... couldn't sleep," she replies, twirling the remote in her hand. "What made you wake up?" He sits on the couch next to her, taking the remote and turning the television off.

"Well, I dreamt that I caught a beautiful angel in my arms, but then she flew away from me." Princess of Havok giggles, blushing. "So I went and tried to find her, and I did. And she was gnawing on a pickle."

"You knew all along, huh?" she asks, embarrassed.

"Your breath told the story," he laughs, patting her leg.

"Thanks."

"But seriously, buttercup. If you get hungry, just go ahead and have something. I won't be angry," Lint explains.

"You were nice enough to let me stay here, and I'm eating you out of house and home."

"Eating me out? But that's not possible!" Princess of Havok laughs and hugs him. "I enjoy taking care of you. And it's not that I can't afford more food. I just figure, why buy more when we can't eat it that quickly anyway?"

"Really?"

"Believe me, punky. I'm not poor," he replies, smiling that gorgeous smile of his.

"Okay. I don't think I'll have a problem sleeping now," Havok announces, pulling Lint up off the couch.

"If you do, just let me know."

The next day at school, Unan prances to her locker with a fresh banana in hand. After twenty minutes, she still doesn't see her sidekick and begins to worry. The usual group of preps gathers to laugh and stare at her. Since Princess of Havok isn't there, she has to come up with something to say to them.

"Go fuck yourselves."

"Yeah right! What do you think *guys* are for? Oh, wait. You, like, wouldn't know!" Obviously, the enemy has become more snappy. Unan is disappointed and has no clue what to say next. Luckily, Dave sweeps past, picking her up and spinning her around in the air. The makeup-faced idiots saunter away, frowning.

"Whee!" Unan cries. When he puts her back on the ground, she tightens her bondage belt by one more notch. Since the heat started, all her clothes seem even bigger, drowning her in excess material.

"Where's Havok?" Unan shrugs and begins to walk down the hallway.

"Maybe she's hanging out with *Veda*," she replies.

"Where are you going so soon?" Dave asks, attempting to follow her.

"Algebra two. I'm not in Calculus like you are."

"But it's still early!" Dave insists.

"I have to get my spot in the back so I can doodle on the wall." She blows him a kiss and giggles. "See you in data processing!"

Princess of Havok wakes up, thinking she couldn't possibly have missed a whole day of school. But it's midnight, and she's still sitting up in bed. Lint enters the room, his mohawk missing and all of his hair the same length, short, bleached spikes.

"Wha—where's all your hair?"

"Gone. How are you feeling?" he asks, concern in his voice.

"Alright. Kinda hungry."

"I can imagine! You haven't eaten all day! Just puked this morning," he announces, grabbing her hand. His grip feels like Alexey's. Sexy Alexey... it seems like forever ago he was writing mini-RPGs for them, and he and Dave hung out every day. Until Russia snatched him away. "Havok? What do you want to eat?"

"Could I have... a pickle?" she whispers. "And some yummy ice cream?" He looks at her in disbelief, his mouth hanging open. "Weird craving?"

"I guess so!" he laughs. "Hella weird." Perhaps even weird enough to make Princess of Havok sick again the next morning, which she was. After school, Dave sits with Unan on the steps outside.

"This is ridiculous," Unan states, a blank expression on her face.

"We still don't know what's going on," Dave replies, people-watching.

"I'll tell you what's going on. She's chilling with that stupid slut."

"Unan..."

"I don't know how she can pull this shit. How can she just up and leave? I... trusted her. Dammit, I barely trust *anyone*."

"I know," Dave says. He tugs on his striped socks and ties his shoelaces.

"Wanna stay over tonight?" she asks, grinning mischievously. He nods.

"Absolutely."

The evening flies by quickly, the coffeehouse lights on now, candles decorating the stage. The people haven't cleared out yet, so Dave and Unan sit at a table, talking and sipping on wine. It's an open mike night, and some loser is up on stage, trying to act like a beatnik. A few girls are sitting on the couch, talking about how "buff" he is. They point in an extremely obvious manner, giggling in high-pitched voices.

"Wanna mess with them?" Unan asks. A twinkle passes across Dave's blue eyes.

"Hell yeah." The jerk wearing a black turtleneck – in the middle of summer – leaves the stage, trying to look intellectual and somber. He struts over to the couch and sits between the girls, putting his arms around their shoulders. They squeal with delight like pigs rolling around in mud. Unan

112

pretends to gag, and Dave laughs as he makes his way over to the stage. He clears his throat in front of the microphone.

"This is called *Contemplating Murder*." He stifles a smile, placing his hand over his mouth. "She smiles. I frown. Two eyes filled with hopes of a bright future. My eyes see only a pathetic, sniveling girl. She says hi. Clueless. I grab the scissors on her desk. She says she can explain, but... I don't believe her." Some people start to leave the coffeehouse, shaking their heads. Dave continues. "She can't make up for what she did. *Nobody* deserves a second chance!" Dave yells. "So what if she begged for mercy, huh?! I still stabbed her with those scissors and gouged her pretty eyes right out of her head!" The coffeehouse is now empty, and Unan has locked the door. However, Dave is not done performing. "Yeah, so that's all. Because I woke up and realized it was all just a dream. Thank you." He bows and jumps off the stage, hugging Unan.

"Well, that was a wonderful... whatever it was," she compliments him, pulling on her pyramid belt.

"Hey, can I have some of that?" Dave asks, tugging on it, too. She giggles, blushing and looking at the floor.

"Stop it. My pants are gonna fall off," she laughs.

"So?" The phone rings, and Unan is about to run and get it, but she can't. He's too beautiful, and she's drowning in his deliciousness. Bright blue punk rawk eyes beckoning her to look into them. The answering machine goes on, distracting them both. When Unan hears Havok's voice, she throws her arms across her chest and begins to tap her foot on the floor, impatiently.

"Unan? Unan!" she whispers, sharply. "Unan, you won't believe me in a thousand years... but, I... I..."

"God, spit it out!" Unan says aloud, to nobody in particular.

"I think I'm pregnant. I don't know what... I mean... I'm so—" The statement is cut off quickly when Havok slams the phone down.

"What did I tell you?" she asks Dave. He looks around for some reason, then takes his shirt off and throws it on the couch.

"Maybe you're right. You gonna call her back?"

"Wasn't planning on it."

"Then why aren't you over here in my arms?" he interrogates, smiling slyly. Unan starts toward him, taking her time. When she gets there, she puts one hand on his wonderful chest, savoring his tan skin. He wraps a strong arm around her waist. "Isn't that better?" Dave whispers. She nods, closing her eyes and waiting for his soft lips to take her to heaven and back. He pauses for a moment to tease her, then grants her wish. Normally, anything foreign like that in her mouth grosses her out. Ryan... he... oh well. Ancient history. Wait. Foreign. Like certain Dave parts. Unan almost giggles at the thought. With Dave, it's okay. She knows him. She loves him.

"I want you," she announces, quietly. He leads her over to the couch and pulls her down on top of him.

"Oh yeah?"

"Yup," she replies. It's not fair that he can be so nice and cooled off without his shirt on, so she whips hers off, too.

"Wow."

"We're equal now," she explains. "Am I hurting you? Just let me know if I'm crushing you or something."

"Sweetie? Your pants fall off if you're not wearing a belt. I'm fine." Dave laughs, thinking of the absurdity of her statement.

When their clothes are all lying on the floor, the coffeehouse seems hotter than before. Dave and Unan are simply resting, her finger tracing his small pecs. He is running a hand down to the small of her back, and then daring to cup her butt in his hand. All of a sudden, Unan jumps up and runs to turn the answering machine off. She comes flying back and stops right next to the couch.

"Are you sure you want to do this?" Dave asks. Unan pretends to think for a moment, then crawls back on top of him. "Mmm." She reaches behind her. "Okay, hello!" She giggles and leans forward, licking Dave's neck. "Alright."

"Wait!" Dave looks at her, confused. "Protection?"

"I've already got it all covered," he replies.

114

"How did I not notice that?!" They both crack up until Unan moves and slides onto Dave.

Meanwhile, Lint watches Princess of Havok sleep, her left hand clutching her stomach. He tries to think of possible causes of her illness, his mind immediately latching onto... but that can't be. They have only done it once. Of course, they weren't safe when they did. He sighs, running a hand through his short hair. The haircut was supposed to be an exciting surprise, but their current predicament dulls any other occurrence.

Getting impatient with himself, Lint stands up and strolls into the kitchen, kicking off his Converse shoes. He opens the refrigerator and peers inside, catching a glimpse of the pickle jar. Holding it up in the air, Lint reads the nutrition label.

Another school day passes. Another disappointment for Unan and Dave. It seems as though they will never get their friend back from the dark side, from the trampy grasp of Veda. Unan is ready to bitch her out, but the whole day, she can't seem to find her. After school, she and Dave look for her outside on the steps.

"I don't even see her anywhere," Unan sighs. She's had time to really think about what it would be like to not have Havok anymore. Her sidekick. Her partner in crime. Nothing could break Xena and Gabrielle apart. Wait... Unan shakes her head. What was *their* idea of a slut? They ran around with barely any clothes on!

"Me, neither," Dave replies. "What's her name again? Veda?"

"Yes?" a girl answers. She's sitting on a stone wall, reading a book called *I Was a Teenage Fairy*. She turns to look at them, peering over her thick, black, geeky frames.

"Wait, you're not Veda. You didn't have glasses the other day," Unan declares.

"I just realized how popular contacts are. Anyway, I can assure you I'm Veda." Unan balls her hands up into fists, breathing heavily.

"Well, good. I can finally tell you to stop warping my friend's mind. You know, I haven't even seen her once since you started taking up all her time!"

Veda puts her book down and watches the funny, stick-skinny girl spaz in front of her. "I can't believe you. And now, poor Havok thinks she made the mother of all mistakes!" Veda still continues to stare, opening her mouth, ready to protest. "She thinks she's preg—Oh, no. You're here, and she's not. Why didn't I realize it?" Unan asks. "You haven't been hanging with her, have you?"

"You stole the words right out of my mouth." She picks her book up once again.

"Oh, shit," Unan mutters.

"I hope your friend is alright," Veda announces.

"You mean... you're not mad that I yelled?" Unan asks, grabbing onto Dave's hand.

"No. I'm not perfect, so I certainly don't expect anyone else to be, either." Unan smiles, hoping they can somehow become friends. "By the way, when you find out how your friend is doing, let me know."

Unan and Dave go to Lint's house to find them sitting in the living room, holding each other and watching TV. They find out that Princess of Havok's been home all along, sick in bed. However, the real reason was pickles that were a little old. Nevertheless, they get everything straightened out, but Princess of Havok has news:

Alexey called, and he wants to come and visit them all.

Another event never to be forgotten. The sun continues to shine, and the war goes on.

www.ingramcontent.com/pod-product-compliance
Lightning Source LLC
Chambersburg PA
CBHW030636130626
46552CB00002B/873